SPIRIT WORLD

SPIRITS AND SPELLS

BRUCE COVILLE

Hodder Children's Books

a division of Hodder Headline plc

To the members of Apanage – past, present and future

First published in the USA in 1996 as an Archway Paperback
entitled *Chamber of Horrors: Spirits and Spells*,
published by Pocket Books, a division of Simon & Schuster Inc.

First published in Great Britain in 1998
by Hodder Children's Books

10 9 8 7 6 5 4 3 2 1

A Catalogue record for this book is
available from the British Library

ISBN 0 340 71459 X

Typeset by Hewer Text Ltd, Edinburgh
Printed and bound in Great Britain

Hodder Children's Books
a division of Hodder Headline plc
338 Euston Road
London NW1 3BH

ABOUT THE AUTHOR

Bruce Coville has been scaring people ever since he was born and the doctor screamed, 'Oh, my God! What's *that*?'

His parents were nearly as terrified.

His teachers are still nervous wrecks.

All that took place back in the totally terrifying decade of the 1950s, in and around Syracuse, New York.

When Bruce became a teenager, his grandfather put him to work digging graves in the local cemetery.

His high school's official colours were orange and black.

He spent as much time as possible watching monster movies, reading Famous Monsters of Filmland magazine, and scaring himself by imagining what might be underneath his bed.

Given all that, we have to ask you: Is it any surprise he writes this kind of book?

Mr Coville now lives with his wife, his youngest child, and their three weird cats in a rather old brick house on a hill in Syracuse.

He hasn't dug a grave in years.

Or so he says.

Also by Bruce Coville
from Hodder Children's Books

Spirit World: Restless Spirits
Spirit World: Eyes of the Tarot
Spirit World: Creature of Fire

Aliens Ate My Homework
I Left Sneakers in Dimension X
Aliens Stole My Dad

Goblins in the Castle

1

"IT'S ONLY A GAME"

When Lydia began to scream, Tansy Parker finally decided it was time to call it a night. "That's enough!" she said, slamming down her pencil. "Travis, stop the game."

Travis Wyman, Tansy's boyfriend, ran a long-fingered hand through his black hair. He opened his mouth to protest, but Tansy had already turned to Lydia. She took the girl by the shoulders and shook her. "Lydia. Lydia, stop it!"

Lydia stopped screaming. She blinked at the others, a dazed expression on her face.

"Tansy! What . . . what happened?"

Tansy smiled uncertainly. "I'm not sure. I think you got too involved with the game."

Lydia put a hand to her brow. "I don't feel well," she said weakly. "I'd like to go home."

Lydia's boyfriend had been watching her with a stunned expression on his face. Jumping to his feet, he said, "That's a good idea!" After wrapping Lydia's sweater and then his own arm around her shoulders, he guided her to the door.

Tansy went with them as far as the porch, where she stood to watch them disappear into the cool October night.

"That was weird," she said when she returned to what was left of the group. Her large hazel eyes, usually clear, were troubled.

"Lydia's weird," said Derek. "She always acts dumb."

Tansy scowled at him. Derek Clarke was so good-looking he often got away with saying unpleasant things. While Tansy enjoyed his sense of humor, his total lack of sympathy for others often made her angry.

"This whole game is weird," said Jenny. Tansy shifted her gaze to Jenny Erickson, Derek's girlfriend. Tansy had always been jealous of Jenny's beauty. Her long blond hair and clear complexion made Tansy resent her own short red curls and freckle-spattered cheeks.

Fortunately, Travis claimed to love freckles.

"The game really *is* weird, isn't it?" said Travis now. His voice was ecstatic; he was hugely satisfied with his discovery, despite Lydia's reaction. "Too bad we didn't have a chance to finish it. But we will next time. I think this may be the greatest game ever."

Tansy sighed. Most of the girls she knew hung around with guys who liked to play football. Somehow she had managed to get interested in a gaming freak. Now while most of her friends were jumping up and down in the bleachers, she was rolling dice and learning about the powers of third-level characters.

Even worse, she was starting to enjoy it! But this new one—Spirits and Spells—was decidedly creepy.

"Where did you find this thing anyway, Travis?" asked Derek.

"At the gaming convention in Pittsfield last weekend. The place was crammed and the table I really wanted to get to had a mob four deep around it. I was trying to decide whether to wait my turn or come back later when I noticed this old guy sitting at a table all by himself. He motioned me over. I didn't go at first—didn't want to lose my place. But finally I got bored and decided to come back to the main table later. So I figured I might as well talk to the old guy. He told me this game was his own invention—that it had come to him in a dream. He was really fierce about that: he called it 'an inspiration from the beyond.' "

Travis laughed. "To tell you the truth, I think he was a little nuts. Anyway, he was trying it out at the convention, to see if it would sell. And nuts or not, I think he's got a real winner. Just think, you guys—if this thing takes off, we'll have been just about the first people in the world to play it. It'll be like being the first to have played Dungeons and Dragons, or Magic."

Suddenly his eyes widened. Grinning broadly, he said, "And I've just thought of the best way to play it!"

"How?" asked Derek, who was always ready for something new.

"Well, the action takes place in a haunted house, right?"

Derek shrugged. "Every game has a setting; a forest, a castle, an island. What's the big—" His eyes widened as he realized what Travis was suggesting. "The Gulbrandsen place!"

Travis nodded smugly.

Jenny shook her head, causing her blond hair to swing over her shoulders. "I don't know, you guys. That place is kind of spooky."

"That's the idea!" said Derek. "This game is *supposed* to be spooky. Oh, man—it'll be a riot." He turned back to Travis. "But how are we going to get into the place?"

"That part is easy. I can get a key from my dad's office. His company is supposed to be selling the property. But there's some kind of fight between the heirs, and until they settle it, no one can buy the place. To tell you the truth, I don't think anyone will ever buy it even if they do settle. No one's even asked to look at it for the last eight months."

Tansy glanced down at the game book. The words *Spirits and Spells* blazed across the top of it in large red letters. Beneath the lettering was a picture of a witch and a warlock with bolts of power flashing out of their hands.

"I don't know," she said slowly. "There's something about this that gives me the creeps."

Travis frowned. "Come on, Tansy. After all . . . it's only a game."

The mocking words earned him a glare. Tansy had used those very words herself countless times during the last year. But that was different. Travis was so wrapped up in fantasy gaming, he sometimes seemed to think it was more real than real life. He could get furiously upset if he thought someone was not playing fairly. Tansy always felt obliged to try to calm him down at those times, and "It's only a game" were the words she usually used to do it.

He smiled, and after a moment she shrugged and grinned, laughing at herself for being afraid. Who could tell? This might be fun after all.

"Okay," she said. "Let's plan on Friday night. But we'll need two more players. Why don't we ask Matt and Denise?"

A dark look flickered across Travis's face. Tansy rolled her eyes in response. It was true that Matt McMasters had been her first boyfriend. But that had been way back in eighth grade. As far as she was concerned, Travis's ongoing jealousy in regard to Matt was just plain stupid.

"Good idea," said Derek, in his usual clueless fashion. "You should have invited them to begin with, Travis."

"I have to call Denise tonight," said Jenny. "I'll ask her then."

Travis sighed, but said nothing.

Jenny winked at Tansy.

Since it was a school night, it wasn't long before the rest of the group decided to leave as well, Travis lingering behind for a good-night kiss.

Tansy was heading for her bedroom when the phone rang.

It was Lydia.

"I just wanted to apologize for tonight," she said. "For breaking things up."

"It's all right," said Tansy, letting her fondness for Lydia overcome her annoyance. "But are *you?* All right, I mean. What happened, anyway?"

Lydia was so silent that for a moment Tansy thought they had been cut off. When she finally spoke, her voice was little more than a whisper. "I felt . . . *fingers.* Icy fingers, probing at my mind. Tansy, tell Travis to get rid of that game. It's dangerous. No, it's not just dangerous. It's evil."

Then she did hang up, leaving Tansy to stare at the receiver and wonder if Lydia was losing her mind after all. She shivered and put the receiver back in its cradle. Lydia was living proof that it really was possible to be too imaginative for your own good.

Even so . . .

Well, it was too late to back out now. Travis would never let her hear the end of it if she did.

Besides, Lydia was just being foolish.

How could a mere game be evil?

2

THE GULBRANDSEN PLACE

Tansy and Travis stood on the sidewalk in front of the Gulbrandsen house. Its huge turrets loomed out from a sky dark with massing clouds. A low rumble of thunder indicated that the storm which had been brewing all day would break soon.

"What do you mean, 'This place really is haunted?' " asked Tansy scornfully. She was already disturbed enough by her conversation with Lydia; she didn't intend to let Travis rattle her with a bunch of nonsense. "All I ever heard was that old Mr. Gulbrandsen died without a will, so the authorities closed the house until the estate could get settled."

"Which won't be for years," said Travis. "With all those greedy second and third cousins squabbling to get their slice, this place will probably fall down before anyone gets a penny out of it. But don't tell me you never heard about the murder?"

His know-it-all attitude was starting to annoy Tansy. "What murder?" she asked sharply.

"The murder of Charity Jones. She was a servant girl who was killed here, way back in the 1800s. No one knows who did it. But it was very violent, very brutal. Her spirit still haunts the place."

"Stop it, Travis."

He shrugged. "Do you want to go in?"

"Why ask me? Even bribing you with a pepperoni pizza couldn't stop you at this point. So I doubt that any second thoughts on my part would slow you down."

He gasped. "Tansy, you cut me to the soul!"

"You'll heal. Now are we going to stand here talking all night or are we going to go in?"

Travis put his hand on the metal gate. "In!"

"Well, lead on, MacDuff."

He grinned at her nervously, then pushed the gate open. The hinges creaked mournfully.

Tansy followed Travis up the walk, which was edged with overgrown shrubs. A sudden gust of cold wind swept dead leaves about their feet, and the steps of the old porch groaned as they climbed them.

Unlike the gate, the door—made of dark wood and ornately carved—swung open without a sound.

"Wow," said Tansy as they stepped through. "This is even better than I imagined!"

Gazing up at the high ceiling and the cobwebbed chandelier, she reached behind her to close the door.

A cold, wet hand closed over hers.

With a scream she snatched her hand away and

darted forward. She hadn't gone more than three steps when she heard a familiar burst of hysterical laughter.

"Derek!" she cried angrily.

Derek Clarke was almost helpless with mirth. "Tansy, you . . . are . . . so much *fun!* I can always count on you for a good reaction."

Tansy was not laughing. She found herself wondering—not for the first time—why she put up with Travis's crazy friends.

Travis didn't seem to be amused, either. "Knock it off, Derek. You'll spoil the atmosphere."

As Derek tried to stifle his laughter, Jenny stepped from the shadows. Tansy saw that she was holding a plastic bag with some ice cubes inside. Well, at least that explained how Derek had made his hand so cold.

"Sorry, Tansy," said Jenny softly. "I told him not to, but . . ." Her voice trailed off.

Tansy knew what she meant. Trying to keep Derek under control was like trying to get cats to march in a straight line.

"Are Matt and Denise here yet?" asked Travis.

Derek shook his head. "Matt called me earlier today and said they would be a little late. I think Denise was having a little trouble convincing her parents to let her come."

Travis frowned. "Well, let's go upstairs and set up. Maybe by the time we're ready, they'll be here."

"Where are we going to play?" asked Jenny.

"In the library," said Travis. "I found it when I came to scope the place out yesterday. It should be perfect for the game."

* * *

The broad, curving stairwell was thick with dust, disturbed only where Travis had walked on his earlier scouting expedition. When Tansy reached for the banister, she found her fingers tangled in a cobweb. Resisting an impulse to squeal, she wiped her hand against her jeans.

As they climbed, the little bit of light that had filtered in from outside faded rapidly.

Derek switched on a flashlight.

The hallway at the top of the stairs was hung with forbidding portraits of generations of Gulbrandsens. If the paintings were accurate, the whole family had had high cheekbones, fierce eyes, and thin, harsh lips.

The carpet that lined the hall was faded but still thick. It muffled their footsteps so that they walked in near silence.

Tansy felt as if the eyes of the portraits were looking down on them with disapproval. The thought made her shiver.

When they entered the library, she relaxed a little. The room was beautiful. Three leaded-glass windows looked out over a rolling lawn that appeared as if it hadn't been mowed all summer. Dark wood shelves covered the other walls, all of them still lined with books. Close to the windows stood a large oak desk. In the center of the room was a long table, oak also, its legs carved to look as if they ended in clawed feet.

Travis stationed himself at one end of the table. He whispered something to Derek, who left the room and came back a minute later with two candelabra. He took some candles from his backpack, set them in the holders, and lit them.

The flickering flames cast an eerie glow over the room.

Travis opened the game box and took out the manuals that came with the set. Totally absorbed, he began writing on a pad, making some calculations.

Jenny and Tansy wandered around the library, examining the old books.

"Boy, the guy who owned this place must have been a real weirdo," said Jenny, running the tip of her index finger over a set of leather-bound volumes. "Here's six whole books on the history of witchcraft in America."

"And here's one called *Lycanthropia,*" said Tansy.

Jenny looked puzzled. "What's that supposed to mean?"

Tansy smiled. "Werewolfism," she whispered ominously.

Jenny shuddered and shook her head. Candlelight caught and shimmered in her pale gold hair. "What kind of people were the Gulbrandsens? Why did they have books like these?"

"Those books are just right for a haunted house," said Derek, walking up behind them. "A place stalked by the spirit of a poor murdered girl."

Jenny slapped his shoulder. "Don't be stupid. If you get me too scared, I'll go home."

"Alone? In the dark?"

Jenny looked uncomfortable. "Stop it. I don't think you're funny."

"I'm not being funny," said Derek.

"That's for sure," said Tansy. "But Travis told me the same thing, Jenny. There was a girl murdered here."

Derek rubbed his hands together and chuckled evilly. "And ever since, on wild and windy nights people have looked up here and seen lights moving through the windows—even when no one was home. Even after the place was abandoned. They say it's Charity Jones, searching for her bones."

Jenny snorted. "You are hopelessly corny."

Derek looked offended. "That's not corny. It's classic."

"It's also true," said Travis, who had joined them while Derek was speaking. "At least the part about the bones is. My grandmother has a clipping in the scrapbook that *her* grandmother kept. I read all about it. The body was never found."

"Well, then, how do they know she was murdered?" asked Tansy sensibly. "She probably just ran away."

"I said they never found the *body,"* answered Travis. "All the killer left behind was her head."

"Euuuw!" cried Tansy.

"Don't be so gross!" said Jenny.

"I'm not being gross. I'm just telling you what happened."

Jenny frowned. "Well, it's still gross."

A crash downstairs made them all jump. Jenny, her face pale, clutched Tansy's arm.

Derek laughed. "Ever graceful, ever silent, McMasters and Wu are here at last. At least, I *presume* that's who it is." He gave his evil chuckle again.

Matt McMasters's voice boomed up from below. "Anybody here?"

"Upstairs!" called Travis, stepping into the hall.

The newcomers bounding up the stairway made an

unlikely couple. Matt was short and intense, standing only slightly over five feet. He had dark hair, dark eyes, and a dark streak in his personality that would have made him unbearable had it not been balanced by a healthy sense of humor.

Denise Wu had dark coloring, too, but she was tall—even taller than Travis. Of the three girls she was far and away the most enthusiastic gamester. Shy and reserved in school (although a straight-A student), she lit up when she was with a group of players. Involvement in gaming was the tie that held her and Matt together.

Right now, her dark brown eyes were glowing with excitement. "It's a perfect night for this," she said in a whisper. "There is one monster of a storm brewing out there."

Just like Denise to be rooting for a real gullywasher, thought Tansy.

"Let's get started," said Travis.

They pulled some chairs over to the library table. Outside, the October evening had plunged into total darkness. The wind was whipping around the house, and branches scratched at the windows. It really was a perfect setting for Spirits and Spells.

Maybe too perfect, thought Tansy nervously.

"You're going to have to go over the rules carefully," said Matt. "You guys have all had a chance to play this, but it's brand-new to me and Denise."

Tansy could tell from Matt's voice that he was annoyed he and Denise had not been invited to the group's first attempt at the game. Of course, he had never noticed that Travis was jealous of him. But that was Matt. His emotional obliviousness was one of the reasons Tansy had broken up with him to begin with.

"We only played for about an hour," said Derek scornfully. "Then Lydia went berserk and we had to stop."

"For heaven's sake, give her a break," snapped Tansy. "She has a lot of imagination. That's what makes her such a great player. She's just got more of it than she can handle."

A moment of awkward silence settled over the table, broken when Travis cleared his throat. The five adventurers looked at him expectantly.

"All right, here's the background," he said, reading from the first manual. "We are powerful magic users, witches and wizards who have been exiled to the world of Quarmix by Mormekull, a mighty wizard who resented our abilities.

"For the hundreds of years we have been trapped here, we have been planning our escape. During this time we have practiced our magic, honed our skills, increased our power.

"Recently we discovered a new source of magic on this world. Now our strength is greater than ever—nearly great enough to enable us to break the spells that hold us here, so we can return at last to Earth.

"But our enemy, Mormekull, has learned that our powers are growing. He fears we will break free, so he has prepared this house as a trap for us."

"What kind of a trap?" asked Matt.

Travis shot him an impatient glance. Tansy squirmed in her seat, fearing a clash between the two boys. But Travis went right on.

"The house is a gateway between the two worlds. It was through this very place that Mormekull first expelled us from Earth.

"Now he is playing a desperate game. Four objects of power are all we need to break the spell and return home. Mormekull has hidden them in the house to lure us back here. If we find them before dawn, he loses, and we are free."

"That doesn't make any sense," said Matt. "If he already has us in exile, why is he giving us a chance to escape?"

Travis smiled. "He is taking this chance because if we fail in our quest he can be rid of us forever. As I said, the house is a trap. It was sealed against our leaving when we entered it."

At that moment the wind slammed against the shutters, closing them over the windows with a bang. Jenny shrieked. Even Travis looked startled. But he went on.

"If we can break the magical barriers, we can leave the house and be free. But if we fail, we are doomed. *Because this house dies at dawn—along with everyone still in it.*"

The words had barely left his lips when a crack of thunder rattled the room.

Jenny jumped again.

Tansy shivered.

Travis laughed.

The game had begun.

3

CLUES

As Travis's laugh died away, a moment of tense silence settled over the library. Jenny twisted a strand of her long blond hair around her finger, looking as though she was about to cry.

Suddenly Denise laughed. "Well, I'd say we're off to a good start! Come on, Trav—what's next?

Tansy relaxed. For a moment she had felt something eerie in the room. Nothing she could put her finger on. Just a sense that all was not right. Denise's cheerful laughter had banished the feeling.

Travis was speaking again. "I have to assign your roles. Matt, you will be the wizard Wathek—"

"Hey! Don't we get to create our own characters?"

"No. The directions are specific. They give the name of each player."

"But that's not the way gaming works," said Matt with a frown. "Making up my own character is one of the things I like best."

Denise looked troubled, too. But she put a hand on Matt's arm. "Let's play it by the rules the first time. We can always change it the next time through. That's the other good thing about gaming. You can change the rules to suit yourself."

"Well, all right," said Matt, none too graciously. "Go on, Travis."

"I'm not Travis. I am Karno, the Master Mage."

"What?"

Travis sighed. "That's *my* role in the game. That's one of the neat things about Spirits and Spells. The game leader gets a character, too. My character is pretty interesting, I think. I know where everything is, but Mormekull has put a spell on me so I can't tell anyone. I can only speak in riddles, to give you clues. We'll get to that in a minute. Now Matt . . . Wathek . . . you have the power to become invisible. You can see spirits, and cast spells of fire and illusion."

Matt nodded, apparently satisfied.

"Tansy, your character is named Theoni."

Tansy took out the small notepad she had brought with her. She always had trouble keeping these things straight at first.

"You are an enchantress who can communicate with spirits. You can compell the truth from anyone except me. You have third-level spells for fire and freezing."

Tansy scribbled furiously in the notepad.

Travis continued assigning roles and powers. Derek

was a wizard named Diaz, who had unusual physical strength. He could sense falsehood and had the power of temporary binding.

"You can stop anyone, or anything," Travis told him. "But only for a brief time. The duration depends on the strength of your foe."

Turning to Denise, he said, "Your name will be Niana."

"Hey, I like that! I think I'll use it from now on. It's a lot classier than Denise."

Tansy smiled. It was a typical Denise reaction.

"You are a healer," continued Travis, "with a song for sleep and soothing. You have spells for frost and flight."

"All right!"

"Come on, Travis," said Jenny. "Tell me who *I* am."

Tansy's smile grew broader. Clearly Jenny was getting into the spirit of the game. That would make the evening go more smoothly.

"Your name is Gwynhafra," said Travis, "and . . . what's the matter?"

Jenny shook her head. "Nothing. It just spooked me for a second. I mean, my name *is* Gwynhafra."

Travis looked totally mystified.

"Jennifer and Gwynhafra are different versions of the same name," Jenny explained, embarrassed. "That's all."

"Oh. Well, you have spells for destroying illusions and opening locks."

"Good. I like those."

"Now, for the first part of the game, you have to locate the objects of power."

Picking up the slender game book, he began to read in low, solemn tones:

> *"A sword, a stave, a rod, a ring;*
> *These emblems of the wizard king*
> *If found before the morning hour*
> *Will free you from the house's power.*
> *Find them and your freedom cherish.*
> *Failure means that all shall perish!"*

Another crack of thunder. Rain began to patter at the windows.

"What's a stave?" asked Jenny.

"A stick," said Travis. "Think of it as a staff, if you want to."

Jenny nodded, satisfied.

"Okay," said Matt. "How do we find these things?"

Travis smiled. "That's what's going to make this game so interesting. The things are really here."

"What do you mean?" asked Derek.

"Yesterday I hid a rod, a ring, a sword, and a stave somewhere in the house. All you have to do is find them."

The five players all began talking at the same time. Finally Jenny stood to make herself heard above the chaos. "You have got to be kidding, Travis! I am not going to go wandering around this place looking for some piece of junk."

"Wait a minute. Wait a minute!" yelled Travis.

"Jenny, I put you and Derek together when I set this up, because I knew you'd be nervous."

"I think it's a fantastic idea," said Denise as Jenny sat down again. "Come on, you guys. Where's your sense of adventure? That's what gaming is all about. This is just one step closer to making it real. Travis went to a lot of trouble. Let's give it a try."

"I'm willing," said Derek.

"Sounds good to me," said Matt.

"Tansy?" Travis looked at her anxiously. Tansy knew that if she took Jenny's side, it would probably end things. She bit her lip. She didn't really want to go wandering around this old place any more than Jenny did. But if she refused, it would hurt Travis's feelings. In fact, they would probably have a colossal fight if she let him down now.

"I'm in," she said, trying to mask her reluctance with a lightness of voice.

Travis smiled at her, and she was suddenly glad she had gone along with the idea.

"Okay, here's how it works. I'll give you guys clues, and you have to figure out where the objects of power are hidden. It's just like playing on paper, except that you actually go look. If you have questions, you'll have to come back here to ask me. But I tried to leave some extra clues around to help you out."

"Oh, and one more thing." Travis gave them a sly grin. "The treasures are guarded."

"What's *that* supposed to mean?" asked Matt.

"It's just like any game," said Travis casually. "Treasures are always protected by something or other."

"Travis, what are you up to?" demanded Derek.

"Trying to set up some fun!" said Travis. His voice sounded hurt. "Do you want to play or not?"

The players eyed him suspiciously. A sense of uneasiness seemed to fill the room. Jenny reached out to touch Derek's shoulder.

But no one got up to leave.

"All right, here are your assignments," said Travis. "First Theoni. Theoni? Hey, Theoni—are you there?"

With a start, Tansy remembered that Theoni was her name for the evening.

"You will be seeking the ring," said Travis. "Here is your clue:

"Closest to heaven, farthest from help,
The wizard's ring lies hidden.
You'll need its power to escape,
So to find it now you're bidden
Face what life has left behind;
Fear not what seems forbidden."

Tansy copied the clue carefully into her notepad.

"Denise, you'll be looking for the rod," continued Travis.

"Call me Niana. And what do you mean by a rod?"

"It's kind of like a magic wand, only bigger," said Travis.

He gave the others their assignments, all of which were in rhyme. A moment of silence followed as the players concentrated on working out the meaning of their clues.

* * *

Tansy read her clue over several times. The first line had struck her when Travis was reading it aloud. "Closest to heaven" could mean the ring was somehow near goodness. Perhaps it was hidden in a family Bible. But then why would it be "farthest from help?" That didn't make any sense.

"Closest to heaven" could also mean "high in the sky." Well, in the Gulbrandsen place, the spot closest to heaven was the attic.

Of course! That would take her farthest from help, and it fit perfectly with the line about "Face what life has left behind." The attic would undoubtedly be filled with the leavings of a lifetime, all the things the Gulbrandsens had collected but never used.

It would probably be very spooky, too.

Tansy frowned. She heard a chair scrape and saw Derek and Jenny get up and head into the hallway. Together. She felt a slight pang. She wished she didn't have to do this on her own.

She glanced at Denise. The dark-haired girl was examining the paper where she had written her own clue. Her brow was wrinkled in concentration, but she didn't show the slightest sign of fear.

Tansy set her jaw. If Denise could do it, so could she. But that dippy Derek had better not try anything funny. She was feeling skittish enough as it was.

Picking up her flashlight, she said, "Well, I'll see you in a little while, Travis. I hope."

"Call me Karno," said Travis. Then he smiled and added, "Good luck, Theoni. Holler if you need me."

She stopped. Narrowing her eyes, she asked, "Are you *expecting* me to holler?"

Travis looked so genuinely innocent she was almost sorry to have been so suspicious.

"No! I was just trying to be nice. See what it gets me?"

"I'm sorry, Travis. *Karno!* I guess I'm kind of nervous."

"Well, that's part of the fun."

"Yeah," said Tansy. "Fun."

She walked out of the library.

The hall was long and dark. She shone the light first to her left, then to her right, where she spotted a stairway. She started toward it.

Another crack of thunder made her jump, and for a moment she considered turning back.

"Come on, Theoni—get a grip," she whispered to herself. She grimaced. If she didn't watch it, she'd end up standing here all night, arguing with herself.

She headed up the stairs.

The third floor of the Gulbrandsen house was quiet and still. The hall was uncarpeted, and dust lay thick over everything. She wondered how to get to the attic. Shining her flashlight down the hall, she caught her breath. Footprints! Then she realized they had to be Travis's, and relaxed.

Well, this would make things easy. All she had to do was follow them. She wondered if he had been careless enough to leave tracks all the way to the ring. Maybe he had swept up after himself farther along to obliterate them. Or maybe not. Tidiness had never been his specialty.

Feeling smug, Tansy followed the footprints along the hall. Aha! Here was the stairway to the attic.

She sighed. The footprints stopped. The steps had been swept clean. She was going to have to work a little harder than she had thought.

She played her flashlight beam up the stairs. At the top was a door, held shut with an old-fashioned latch.

Tansy took a deep breath and started up the stairs.

4

THE DEPTHS

Derek and Jenny stood at the top of the main stairway, the curving one they had first climbed from the foyer. They watched as Tansy moved to the other end of the hall and disappeared up the next flight of stairs.

Jenny shivered. "I don't know how she can do it."

"Do what?"

"Go looking for that ring on her own. I'd be petrified."

"That's why you're with me," said Derek with a smirk.

"And I'm still petrified." She aimed her flashlight down the stairs and shuddered.

"Come on, Jen—I'll be right beside you all the time."

"Why do you think I'm so scared!"

Derek scowled. "Thanks a lot!"

"Oh, Derek—you know I'm kidding. But I still don't like it here."

"Look, Travis assigned us together to keep you from getting into a panic. What more do you want?"

"To go home."

"Forget it. We're playing out the game."

She sighed. "All right, O fearless one—what do we do next?"

"Did you write down the clue?"

Jenny flipped her golden hair over her shoulder. "Of course!"

She took out her pad and read:

"Mighty powers has the sword
That once was stolen from dragon's hoard;
Stolen once, now lost again,
Hidden from the eyes of men,
It's guarded by the earth—and more.
Seek it now to earn your score."

She frowned. "What's all that supposed to mean?"

"Well, it's pretty clear we have to find a sword—a magical sword, which makes sense, considering the game. It was held by a dragon for a long time, then someone stole it from the dragon. Now it's been hidden again, 'deep from the eyes of men.'" Derek smiled. "Heck, this is almost too easy. It has to be in the cellar."

"In the *cellar?* Oh, Derek, I don't think I want to go into the cellar of this place. Besides, what does that line about 'guarded by the earth—and more' mean?"

"That just reinforces that the sword is hidden in the cellar. Cellar—guarded by the earth. Get it?"

Jenny frowned. "I'm not stupid, Derek. I got the part about the earth. It's the 'and more' that has me worried."

Derek paused. "Hmmmm. That's a good point. Travis may have a little surprise planned for us. I wonder if he's planted some friends down there to try to give us a scare."

Jenny stopped in her tracks. "God, I hope not."

"Oh, I do," said Derek eagerly. "Two can play at that game, you know." He grabbed Jenny's hand and pulled her after him. "Come on. We've got to find the cellar door."

They continued down the stairs together, their flashlights cutting a path through the gloom. When they reached the bottom, Jenny swung her beam around the spacious foyer. "Which way now?" she whispered.

"Let's try over there," said Derek, pointing to their left. "Looks like a pretty big room."

As they passed through the door, Jenny again played her light around the room.

Derek let out a low whistle. "Did I say big? This place is like a cavern!"

At the far end of the room loomed a huge fireplace. Its chimney, made of gray stone, took up half the wall. The wall to their right, the front wall of the house, had a row of windows masked by dark floor-to-ceiling draperies, thick and heavy. Ghostly, misshapen forms were scattered across the room—the furniture, covered by protective sheets.

"No cellar door here," said Derek after Jenny had played her beam across all four walls. "Just that arch in the back wall."

Moving slowly, they threaded their way among the shrouded pieces of furniture. The arch led into a dining room. A long table stretched before them. Several large paintings hung on the walls.

To the left was another door.

It led to a vast, gloomy kitchen.

"I'll bet the cellar door is in here somewhere," said Jenny, getting caught up in the search in spite of herself. "It would make sense, in a fancy place like this. After all, they wouldn't have it leading out of the living room."

Derek spotted a windowless door against the left wall. Taking Jenny by the hand, he crossed the room and opened it.

"This is it, all right."

Jenny shuddered. The spiderwebs arching over the steps were so thick and numerous they made the passage look more like a tunnel than a stairway. Derek shone his flashlight down it, but they couldn't see the cellar floor.

"There's a broomstick back there," he said. "Grab it for me, will you?"

Jenny moved away from him reluctantly. She found the broomstick lying on a counter beneath a shuttered window and took it to Derek.

"I'll clear a path for us," he said. Moving slowly, he extended the broomstick before him and swung it in wide circles, catching the cobwebs and winding them around the wood like cotton candy around a paper cone.

"No footprints on the steps," he noted. "Of course, there could be another entrance. Or Travis could have been sneaky enough to sprinkle some dust and dirt across the steps behind him."

Jenny reached out and put a hand on Derek's shoulder. A step creaked beneath his sneakers, and she tightened her grip. Derek laughed.

The stairway was longer than she would have expected, and the air grew cooler as they continued down.

"We're almost there," he said. "I can see bottom."

The cellar itself was almost as heavily cobwebbed as the stairway had been. They stood at the base of the stairs and panned their flashlights over dirt floors, thick wooden beams, and millions of clinging webs. The dank air smelled of mold and decay.

"Derek . . ."

"It's all right, Jen. Let's see. Usually at this point in a game we would ask some questions of the leader. He'd probably tell us we should beware of some supernatural menace. But I'm not about to go all the way up to the library just to ask Travis a question. Be careful, though. Like I said, he may have planted something."

"Like what?"

"I don't know. I can't imagine him getting anyone to wait down here to scare us. The place is just too gross. Maybe he set up some water balloons. If we break one and come back all wet, he can say that we stumbled into a trap so we're dead, or under a spell, or something like that."

"That's pretty clever," said Jenny. "But I don't like it."

"Then be careful. Now, shall we split up, or stick together?"

"You have to ask?"

"Not really. Stay with me—and keep your eyes open."

Derek moved forward, still using the broomstick to clear the way ahead of him. He walked slowly, training the beam of his flashlight from side to side, looking for any sign of where Travis might have hidden the sword.

"Derek."

"What?"

"I hear something."

"Jenny, don't get—"

"Just listen, will you?"

Derek heaved an exaggerated sigh. But he stopped to listen.

After a moment his eyes widened. "You're right!" he whispered.

Jenny couldn't tell if it was fear or excitement that made his voice husky.

"It's someone breathing," he went on.

"It's awfully loud breathing," she whispered back.

"Then it's meant to scare us. Brace yourself. He may have someone down here wearing a mask or something. Try not to scream too loud."

Jenny slapped his shoulder. "Try not to wet your pants, smart mouth."

Despite her brave words, she had begun to tremble.

Oblivious to her fear, Derek drew her forward, toward the sound. It was slow and rasping, as if the breather were having real difficulty.

"I don't understand why we haven't spotted footprints," whispered Derek. "He must have come in by some other door."

They moved very slowly.

The breathing got louder.

Derek wrinkled his nose. "Something stinks."

Jenny shifted the beam of her flashlight, found the source of the breathing, and began to scream.

5

THE STAVE

Matt McMasters picked his way slowly through a room he assumed had once been the Gulbrandsen family's den. He was looking halfheartedly for the mysterious stave and wishing wholeheartedly that he and Denise had been kept together, like Derek and Jenny.

It wasn't that he was frightened by being alone. He simply preferred being with Denise.

Wondering if he was kidding himself, he flicked off his flashlight and stood in the darkness, just to be sure.

No, he wasn't afraid. With a sigh, he admitted to himself just how important Denise was to him.

"Rats," he said, flicking his light back on. "Just what I always wanted—a girlfriend who makes me look like one of the seven dwarves."

His eye was drawn to something strange in the corner. It took him a moment to realize it was one of those umbrella stands made from an elephant's foot.

"Good thing Tansy can't see that," he muttered, thinking of the animal-rights pamphlets she used to give him to read.

Moving closer, he realized that the relic contained a selection of canes and walking sticks. "I bet that's it!" he crowed. "One of those has to be the stave!"

He crossed the room eagerly. If he could accomplish his task quickly enough, he could scoot up to the third floor and help Denise with her quest.

The elephant's foot held nearly a dozen sticks, some a mere three feet long, others nearly as tall as Matt himself.

But which was the stave he was supposed to bring back?

He hesitated for a moment, then turned the container over. The sticks clattered out, spilling across the floor. One of them, a polished piece of wood about five feet long, had a white tag fluttering from the end of it.

Matt snatched it up and began to grin. The tag was tied to it with coarse thread. Printed neatly on the tag in red ink were the words "Congratulations. You have completed the first part of your quest. Return to the Master Mage."

Matt started for the door, then turned back. Feeling like an idiot, he set the elephant's foot upright again, then replaced the sticks. "Mom would be so proud," he muttered.

When he reached the second floor, Matt hesitated.

If he went back to the library, he would probably be the first back, which might earn him bonus points.

On the other hand, he really wanted to go help Denise.

"Sorry, Travis," he said, turning to head for the stairs that led to the third floor. The dark hall was eerie, and Matt found himself walking very quietly.

He had nearly reached the stairwell when he cried out in surprise and dropped the stick.

It was hot!

"What's going on here?" he demanded.

He bent and cautiously touched the stick. It was very hot indeed. In fact, it seemed to be glowing faintly.

He sat back on his haunches and stared at the piece of wood. What had Travis done to make it heat up like that? Well, whatever the gimmick was, the stick was too hot to touch. He would have to find something to wrap it in. He stood and cried out in shock a second time.

Two men were standing on the stairs. They were dressed in dark breeches and leather armor, and each carried a long sword. They were looking straight at Matt. One of them opened his mouth and said something.

Matt blinked in surprise. He couldn't hear a thing.

The man moved his mouth again. He seemed to be getting angry.

The second man, small but very muscular, began to walk down the steps. He was gesturing toward the stave, which was lying where Matt had dropped it.

Wathek! cried a voice in his mind. *Don't let them have it!*

Without thinking, Matt snatched up the stave, then cried out in pain. It was still hot.

Suddenly the heat didn't matter. The man who had been heading for the stave lunged at Matt with his sword. Matt bellowed and held up the stave to protect himself. The sword struck it with a jolt that sent a shock through Matt's whole body.

"Denise!" he cried. "Denise, help!"

The stave grew hotter in his hands.

Wathek! whispered the voice in his mind. *Resist them!*

Where was the voice coming from? He had no time to think about it now. The other man was on the attack as well, and it was all Matt could do to fend off their swords with the stave, which was glowing brighter by the second.

6

IN THE ATTIC

Tansy stood at the top of the stairs and took a deep breath. Her mind had begun to conjure up visions of all kinds of horrors waiting on the other side.

She shook herself. This was ridiculous. Despite what Lydia had said, Spirits and Spells was only a game.

Then why was she so frightened?

"Well, it only makes sense," she said out loud, to bolster her courage. "Big old house, stormy October night . . ."

As if to reinforce her words, a crack of thunder shook the walls. Tansy gasped. It was so loud! Taking another deep breath, she put her hand on the latch.

"It's now or never," she said grimly, and swung the door open.

The attic was enormous. It covered the entire house,

so it had as much floor space as all the rooms on the top floor put together. Tansy stepped in, closing the door behind her. She could hear rain pounding on the roof. It seemed oddly close.

She played her flashlight around the attic. Its beam was too weak to reach the far end, but she could see that the place was a jumble of boxes, crates, and trunks. Furniture was piled here and there. On the wall to her right were two bookcases crammed with moldering volumes, the overflow stacked all around. A book lover at heart, Tansy could never pass a pile of books without at least a quick glance at the titles. She went over to look.

A brief scan of the first shelf convinced her there was nothing here that would appeal to her tastes. *Magic and Ritual in New Guinea,* read the spine on the first volume; *The Forbidden Spells,* the second; *Witchcraft in the Middle Ages,* the third.

Tansy grimaced. "Give me a good romance any day," she muttered.

What was that?

She would have sworn she had heard a faint sound, almost like a whisper.

She spun about and swung her flashlight slowly from right to left. "Who's there?" she asked in a shaky voice.

No answer, save the rain pounding on the roof.

She held her breath for a moment, then let it out slowly. Her imagination had been playing tricks on her.

Remembering what had brought her here in the first place, she took out her notepad and reread the clue.

Nothing about it seemed to indicate any specific place in the attic. But Travis had said he had tried to leave some extra clues. She figured she might as well take a moment to look before going back to ask the Master Mage for more information.

She turned back toward the center of the attic. A clear path led from the door where she had entered all the way to the far side of the house. "Sort of like the Red Sea when Moses and the gang went through," she said, surveying the aisle that stretched between piles of relics and discards. The clutter formed two walls that looked likely to collapse and engulf her at any time.

Tansy walked slowly along the path, swinging her flashlight to the right and left. A battered armchair. An old oil painting of a herd of cows, its ornate frame chipped in several places. A dressmaker's dummy, its semihuman form eerie in the gloom.

"This is ridiculous," she said. "How could anybody expect to find a ring in all this mess?"

Was that a noise?

She stopped and listened intently for a moment, then shook her head. She hadn't really heard anything. But she had the uncanny sensation that someone else was in the attic with her—someone waiting, watching to see what she would do.

Tansy wondered if Travis had planted someone here to scare her. She was aware that one good scream, one form leaping unexpectedly from the shadows, would have her shrieking and running for the door.

She walked on, more nervous now, shining her

beam from side to side, looking for any clue to the ring's hiding place.

The rain continued to drum against the roof. Save for her own footsteps, it was the only sound she heard.

Yet she couldn't shake the feeling that she was not alone.

"Travis?"

No answer.

She turned.

"Matt? Denise?"

No answer.

She turned back. As she did, she heard a faint creaking sound several feet ahead of her. Her breath caught in her throat. Her heart felt as if a cold hand had closed about it. There *was* someone here!

Well, if Travis or one of his dopey friends was waiting ahead to jump out at her, she would be prepared. And if she was careful and quiet . . .

She smiled at the thought of turning the tables and surprising whoever it was that waited to scare her.

She walked forward more carefully now, trying to put her feet down silently. The creaking continued, slow and rhythmic. She stopped again. She had thought at first that the sound was being made by someone stepping on a loose board. But it was too regular for that.

What could it be?

She was more than halfway to the far end of the attic now. She could see the gray stones of the chimney.

The creaking continued. Suddenly Tansy lost all interest in trying to surprise whoever might be waiting for her. "Travis? Travis, if that's you, get out here now!"

No answer.

The rhythmic creaking continued.

Tansy bit her lip and considered turning around and heading back. But that might be the very thing the person making the sound, whoever it was, was waiting for. As soon as she turned her back, he would leap out with a shout, scare a good scream out of her, and then laugh like crazy.

She had no intention of letting someone spook her that way. Then she had another thought: Perhaps the creaking was the additional clue Travis had said she would find, and it was *meant* to lead her on. She'd look like a real ditz if she went back to the library without having investigated.

Taking a deep breath, she continued forward.

The beam of her flashlight picked out a fascinating jumble of trash and treasures that, under normal circumstances, she would have loved to stop to examine: a white porcelain elephant nearly three feet tall, a cardboard box overflowing with old clothing and hats, and, ahead of her, a richly patterned Oriental rug, spread out at full length on the floor.

Tansy stopped. The area around the rug was set up almost like a room. The piles of discards around it were like walls. And several pieces of furniture stood on it—a bed, a love seat, and . . .

Tansy gasped. She had found what was making the creaking sound.

The third piece of furniture was a rocking chair.

It was rocking all by itself!

Tansy stood for a moment, unable to move. The chair continued to rock back and forth, making the now familiar creaking sound.

It's a trick!

As soon as the thought flashed through her mind, she could feel her pounding heart begin to slow. Travis had said that the treasures would be guarded. He had set this up. One of his friends was making the chair rock, pulling a string or something.

No. Knowing Travis, he had probably gone all out and connected the chair to a small electric motor. She had watched him tinker with such things before. He was clever enough to arrange something like this with no problem at all.

Feeling considerably more at ease, Tansy headed for the chair, looking for the string she knew had to be attached to it. Or maybe it was fishing line; that would be harder to see.

She had to hand it to Travis. He had done a nice job. The whole idea of setting up a space like a little room, as if someone were actually living here, was truly spooky. And the moving chair with its slow creaking sound had really gotten her going.

The rug was thick and plush, its colors rich even in the light of her flashlight. She stopped for a moment and watched the chair rock. Yes, it had to be a motor making it move with such relentless regularity.

She crossed to the chair, bent to examine it, and felt a sudden chill. She let out a little cry of surprise and stood straight, her heart beating wildly.

It wasn't a cold draft she had felt. Something else

cold waited here, a penetrating cold that reached inside her.

She looked around frantically.

Then, from the empty rocker, came a voice.

"Don't be afraid, miss. I won't hurt you."

Tansy screamed. Her flashlight fell from her hand, hit the carpet with a dull thud, and went out—leaving her in total darkness.

7

VOICES

Denise Wu was scared. She had made her way through several of the third-floor bedrooms without finding the rod, and now the game—the house, the storm, the whole situation—was beginning to get to her.

Standing in yet another doorway, she shook her head, trying to dispel her fear. This was what she had wanted after all: to get really, deeply involved with the fantasy, to live in it—*feel* it. A little fear was part of what everyone was after in gaming. Or maybe a lot of fear. Anyway, she shouldn't complain. It was just the kind of excitement she had been looking for.

She smiled as she thought back to her first experience with fantasy gaming. A pretty girl who happened to be wildly imaginative, Denise was constantly beseiged with requests for dates. Unfortunately, she found most of the boys who asked her out excruciatingly boring, so she usually turned them down. Her mother, a social being if there ever was one, constantly chastised her for being all wrapped up in her own little world.

Denise had to admit that that was true. She just wasn't sure it was all that bad. She sure as heck liked her own world better than the world around her.

Then one day Matt McMasters had invited her to a gaming session, and it had been instant love. Not between her and Matt; between her and fantasy gaming.

Her fondness for Matt had grown more slowly, though now it was strong indeed. The biggest thing they had in common was that they were different. Very different from each other, actually, but alike in being so different from most kids their age. They shared the experience of being outcasts. It was the one thing about the other that each understood perfectly.

Denise wished she were with Matt now. Even though she had felt flattered when Travis sent her off to search on her own, rather than teaming her up with her boyfriend as he'd had to do with Jenny, these eerie, empty rooms had started to seriously spook her.

She crossed the hall and stepped into another bedroom.

Niana.

The voice was a mere whisper, so soft she wasn't entirely certain she had heard it.

But the back of her neck was tingling.

She turned around, saw no one. But suddenly she

felt as if something, someone, was trying to get inside her head.

"Hey!" she shouted. "Stop that!"

But the voice went on whispering to her: *Niana, come back to us!*

Denise bit the back of her hand. This voice was no trick of Travis's, was not coming from some hidden speaker tucked in a corner of the room.

It was inside her head!

Niana . . .

It was a woman's voice, soft and low.

Denise wanted to run but couldn't force her legs to move.

Niana . . .

She felt a scream creeping up her throat. She tried to will it into the open. Maybe if she could scream, someone would come for her.

But no sound would pass her lips.

It was someone else's fear that saved her, when the voice in her head was drowned out by a desperate shout of "DENISE!"

Matt's urgent cry jolted Denise out of her trance.

"Denise! Help me!"

Breaking free of the mysterious voice in her mind, Denise bolted from the room.

Matt's cries seemed to be coming from the stairwell. Denise raced along the hall. When she reached the top of the stairs, she stopped short.

Matt was standing halfway up the stairs, swinging a glowing stick. He was obviously terrified and in need of help. And Denise wanted passionately to provide it.

But how could she help him fight something she couldn't see?

Tansy dropped to her knees and began scrabbling across the attic floor for her flashlight. She would have run, but the darkness was so complete she had no idea which way to go.

"Oh, don't be afraid, miss," said the voice in the rocking chair.

Tansy stopped her searching.

"What?"

"I said don't be afraid."

It was a girl's voice, soft and gentle.

Tansy held her breath.

"Are you all right, miss?" asked the voice.

"I don't know. Are . . . are you a ghost?"

A ripple of laughter, sweet and liquid, greeted the question. "Of course," said the voice. Then it sang.

Charity Jones has lost her bones
And doesn't know where to find them.

Tansy began to shake. It couldn't be. And yet . . .

The voice laughed again. At the same time Tansy's hand brushed against the flashlight. She snatched it like a drowning person grabbing a lifesaver. She gave it a good shake and was relieved when the light turned back on.

The chair was still rocking.

She could see no string.

She began to crawl backward, away from the chair.

"Oh, please don't go, miss."

The voice had responded to her movements. So it was no tape recorder.

Tansy felt the hair on the back of her neck begin to stand up. She wanted to turn and run, but her legs would not obey her command.

The voice spoke again. "I've been so lonely all these years. Won't you stay and talk a bit?"

Rooted to the floor, petrified, Tansy gazed at the rocking chair. Almost without volition, her mouth opened and she found herself asking, "Who are you?" Mixed with her fear was a delicious sense of fascination. She was having a conversation with a ghost!

"I'm Charity Jones, miss. Charity Jones, the murdered maid." The ghost began to sing again. " 'Charity Jones has lost her bones . . .' That's what the children used to sing, after the murder. And it's true."

"What do you mean?"

"Why, just what the song said. I can't find my bones. All I have is what's in that box by the bed. But it's not enough."

Tansy saw a good-sized wooden box on the nightstand beside the bed. "Not enough for what?"

"To free me. Go ahead—take a look."

Tansy walked over and picked up the box. Ornate carvings of elephants and tigers covered the top and sides.

"Be careful!" said Charity Jones's voice.

Tansy opened the box and began to scream.

Inside, staring up at her with sightless eyes, was the perfectly preserved head of a young woman—a girl, really, probably no older than Tansy. She wore a maid's cap. Her face was framed with lovely golden curls. The eyes were blue, with long lashes. Only the pale cheeks and lips were touched by death. Tied around the neck was a scarlet ribbon. Though it was torn and ragged at the edge, no flesh or bone showed beneath it.

Tansy dropped the box.

It landed on the bed. The head fell out and began to roll toward the edge of the mattress.

"Catch it!" screamed Charity Jones.

Responding automatically, Tansy reached out and grabbed the head before it could fall to the floor.

She was instantly aware of what she held in her hands. It was heavy, the hair silky beneath her fingers, the dead flesh smooth and cool.

Screaming again, Tansy dropped the grisly object onto the quilt.

It bounced once, then lay still, face up, staring at her.

"Please, miss, put it back," said Charity.

"What?" Tansy tucked her hands into her armpits to try to stop their violent shaking.

"Put it back in the box. That's my most prized possession. But then, I always was too fond of my looks, according to my mother. Well, just put it back and we'll pretend this never happened."

"I *can't!*" said Tansy desperately.

"Now, miss—it isn't going to bite you. After all, it hasn't opened its mouth in more than a hundred years!"

"But . . ."

"You *are* the one who dropped it. And there you stand with two good hands, which I haven't had in ever so long. So why shouldn't you put it back for me?"

Tansy no longer felt she could refuse. She turned back to the bed. Her stomach lurched, and she thought for an instant she was going to be sick. Steeling herself, she reached down and picked up the head. The hair was soft to the touch.

Gently she placed Charity's head back in the box.

"Turn it just a bit to the right, if you would, miss," said Charity. "So my good side shows a bit more."

Tansy adjusted the head. "Is that all right?"

"Yes, just fine. Thank you."

With a shudder of relief, Tansy closed the box and put it back on the nightstand.

Once she saw that the thing clutching the sword was not moving, Jenny stopped screaming. Derek, recovering from the initial shock, pried her fingers from his biceps.

"If you're going to grab me whenever you get scared, I wish you'd cut your fingernails," he said.

She let go of his arm. "What is that thing?"

Derek shrugged. "The guardian of the treasure, I guess. It's a model of some kind. A dummy. I don't know how Travis managed to make it, but that's what it is."

Jenny pointed her flashlight directly at the monster and examined it in detail. It had a squat, rounded body that ended in several long tentacles, somewhat like an octopus. But that was where the resemblance ended. Its head was split by a wide gash of mouth that was filled with jagged teeth. Above that, two slits, fringed by a loose membrane, formed the hint of a nose.

It was not the mouth or the nose that made Jenny shudder, though. It was the eyes. They were bright and glossy, and except for their abnormally large size—and the fact that one was lower than the other, tilted down as if the flesh had somehow melted around it—she would have sworn that they belonged to a human being.

The reddish brown skin glistened with slime, which had collected on the floor like clotting blood.

Jenny felt sick. "If Travis made that thing, there's something wrong with him."

"We always knew that," answered Derek, forcing a laugh.

"What's making the breathing sound?"

"A tape recorder. Either that, or he's got the thing miked."

"And the smell?"

"I'd rather not think about it. But take a look at the sword. Where do you suppose he got *that?*"

"I don't know," whispered Jenny. "But you're right: It's beautiful."

The golden hilt caught the rays of their flashlights, and fires seemed to spark from the gems encrusting it.

"I'll grab it, and we can get out of here," said Derek, moving forward. "We'll have to be sure to congratulate Travis on what a sick mind he has."

"Be careful!"

Derek snorted in disgust. "Come on—Travis did a good job on the thing, but it's not going to hurt me."

"I know, but—"

Jenny was cut short as Derek slipped on the slime and crashed to the floor.

"Derek! Are you all right?"

He shook his head. "Yeah, I guess so. But this stuff is really—"

"DEREK!"

Derek looked up and let out a bloodcurdling yell.

The creature's tentacles were slithering toward him.

"Get out of there!" screamed Jenny.

Derek pulled his legs underneath him and tried to stand. But his feet slipped in the slime, and he went down again.

The tentacle was coming closer.

"Jenny, help me up!"

But Jenny was screaming, because she had seen what Derek still could not. At the sound of his voice, the creature's great eyes had begun to blink. Suddenly they seemed to focus on Derek.

With a horrible sucking sound the thing pulled itself off the floor and lurched in Derek's direction.

8

TENTACLES

Charity Jones was in her rocking chair again, rocking slowly back and forth. Tansy was sitting on the rug near where she supposed the ghost's feet must be. She found herself wishing she could actually see the dead girl.

"It was a terrible thing, miss," said Charity sadly. "It's not easy to talk about, even now."

"Well, you don't have to, if you don't want to," said Tansy. "I mean—"

"No. It's good to be able to talk about it, if you don't mind listening."

"I'd like to know what happened," said Tansy truthfully.

Charity sighed and Tansy could almost see her settling back into the chair to begin her story.

"It all started when the Gulbrandsens hired me as a serving girl. That was back in, oh, 1888.

"It didn't take me long to figure out I had gotten myself into a strange house. Old Mr. Gulbrandsen was all wrapped up in magic and secret things. I never should have stayed, miss, and that's a fact. It was the first wicked thing I did. If my mother had had any idea what was going on here—witches' sabbaths, strange experiments, all sorts of things—she'd have wanted me to get out. But I hadn't been in this country long, and I was happy to have any work at all."

"So what happened?" asked Tansy.

"Well, Mr. Gulbrandsen had a young friend, a Mr. Morley, who used to come and visit him. One of my jobs was to bring them brandy and cigars in the library." Charity's voice dropped to a confidential whisper. "They usually stopped talking when I came in. It made me wonder what they were discussing. So I started to listen outside the door. They were always talking about 'dark forces' and 'forbidden secrets.' Sometimes I would see pictures they had drawn on the floor—big shapes like stars, with things written at the corners. And they burned candles and incense.

"I knew it was wrong, miss. But what could I do?

"Now Mr. Morley, he had a lady friend. And if you think Mr. Gulbrandsen and Mr. Morley were strange, you should have seen *her*. She could have been the wife of the devil himself. Except she wouldn't have agreed to that, because she was madly in love with Mr. Morley.

"And now I have to make my worst confession. I fell in love with Mr. Morley, too."

"What was so bad about that?" asked Tansy, who always liked a touch of romance in her stories.

"Why, he was a magician—a heathen who worshipped dark powers. Not only that, he was promised to another. And we were of different worlds. He was a wealthy man. I was only a poor serving girl. I had no business being in love with him.

"But it wasn't all my fault. He was the one who started it. Oh, he used to say the dearest things. I tried to put him off and keep him out of my mind. But after a while I was thinking about him more and more."

"That kind of thing happens," said Tansy, feeling wise beyond her years.

"Thank you, miss. I knew you would understand. Not like *her*. She didn't understand anything. One day she caught Mr. Morley kissing me. She was *furious*. And that was the end of me."

An enormous flash of lightning interrupted the story. Its bluish glare flickered through the window at the end of the attic. Thunder followed close and strong, a clap that shook the house on its foundations.

Charity sighed.

"It was a night just like this when that woman came sneaking into this house. I had gone to my little room to try to sleep. Suddenly I heard a sound in the hall. Then the door flew open. There was a flash of lightning, just like now, and I saw her standing there, clutching a big knife."

Charity's voice was low and husky, and the terrified thrill in it made Tansy shiver.

"Well, I saw the knife go up and come down. I felt a horrible flash of pain, a slicing feeling. And that was the last I knew for a time. The next thing I remember, she was gone, and Mr. Morley was there. Poor Mr. Morley. He was crying and calling my name. That made me feel good—to know he really cared about me. Then he knelt beside my bed and began to whisper, 'Charity. Oh, Charity. My poor, poor Charity.'

"That made me feel even better, until I understood why he was so upset."

Charity paused dramatically.

"Why *was* he so upset?" cried Tansy.

"Because I was dead! I mean, there I was, looking at poor Mr. Morley, and I suddenly realized that I was sort of floating above it all, hanging somewhere near the ceiling. Then I saw my head, lying there on the bed. Oh, it was terrible, miss. All that blood. Blood everywhere, and my body nowhere to be seen. Just my head. And Mr. Morley stroking my hair and moaning, 'Oh, my poor Charity. My poor, poor Charity.'

"Well, it turned out my dearie knew more magic than I thought. He and Mr. Gulbrandsen fixed my head up so it wouldn't go bad, if you know what I mean. Then they put it in that box. Mr. Morley used to come here and look at it. But we never found my body. They looked for it everywhere. I was looking, too, though they didn't know that. But I was desperate to find it, because I couldn't leave here until I was buried proper."

"Is that why you're still haunting this place?" asked Tansy.

"Of course it is! Oh, miss, I do wish I knew where that terrible woman put the rest of me. I'm so tired of being bound to this earthly plane. I feel trapped, if you know what I mean. And I've been so lonely."

Moved by Charity's plight, Tansy said, "I have some friends here with me tonight. Would you like to meet them?"

"I surely would!"

"We're gathering down in the library. Come with me."

"Lead the way, miss. I'll be right behind you!"

As Tansy left the attic, she was deep in thought about the best way to introduce Charity to the others. But when she reached the foot of the stairs, her thoughts were disrupted by a loud commotion. She recognized Matt's voice, crving out in anger. Then she heard another voice, deep and rough, and the sound of clanging swords.

Without thinking, she raced forward, only to stop in shock at the next flight of stairs. Matt was shouting and swinging a glowing stick. At first she thought he had lost his mind and was battling thin air.

Then she heard a cry of rage from his invisible enemy.

Mouth working hungrily, the grotesque guardian of the sword had almost reached Derek, who was scrambling along the floor, away from the slippery puddles. But as he struggled to stand, he felt a thick tentacle wrap itself about his ankle.

"Jenny! Help me!"

With a shriek Jenny flung her flashlight at the creature. It struck the monster with a dull thud, fell to the floor, and rolled away. Unbroken, it continued to cast a dim light over the scene.

Derek was trying to pry the tentacle off his leg, but his fingers couldn't get a grip on its slimy surface. At the same time, and unseen by him, another tentacle was slithering forward. The tip of it touched his arm, then began to wind about his wrist.

The creature made a sound of triumph. It began pulling Derek toward its mouth, making an urgent gasping noise, a wheezing cough of hunger.

Derek clawed at the rough cellar floor, trying so hard to drag himself away that he was shredding his fingertips. Suddenly his hand closed on the broomstick he had been using to knock down cobwebs. With a cry of triumph he raised it over his head, then smashed it against the tentacle that still gripped his leg.

With a horrible shriek the creature released Derek's leg. The injured tentacle slithered back across the floor, and the creature popped it into its mouth like a burned fingertip. The bulbous body began to shake and swell. Breath rasping in and out, the monster made a strange burbling noise.

Derek wrenched off the tentacle that still had a grip on his arm, then scrambled backward, his eyes wide. After a moment he shot a wondering glance at Jenny and said, "I think it's trying to *talk!*"

The creature looked straight at Derek. "Thakin obbovver cangoo in retruble!" it said emphatically.

Jenny staggered back against the wall. "You're right! It *is* trying to talk to us."

Removing the bruised tentacle from its mouth, the creature bellowed, "Of course I'm talking. What I said was, 'That kind of behavior can get you in real trouble!' "

Derek was so startled he dropped the broomstick, which clattered to the floor.

The creature raised another, undamaged, tentacle and shook it at him admonishingly. "Look, I don't want to hurt you. But it's my job to guard this sword." Its voice was deep and oddly solemn, with a slight bubbling quality, as if it were coming through a layer of oil.

Derek pushed himself to his feet and went to stand protectively in front of Jenny. She put a hand on his shoulder. "What's going on?" she asked, her voice quivering.

"I don't have the slightest idea what's going on!" shouted the creature, as if Jenny had addressed it and not Derek. "I was sleeping peacefully in my cave when suddenly I woke up and saw him heading for my sword. So I grabbed him. That's what I'm *supposed* to do, you know."

Jenny tightened her grip on Derek's shoulder. "What . . ." She stopped, swallowed, and tried again. "What world are you from?"

"Quarmix. Why?"

Derek blinked in surprise. Quarmix was the world of the game—the supposedly imaginary world where they were playing this all out!

Jenny tightened her grip on Derek's shoulder. "I'm scared," she whispered.

Derek put his hand over hers. "Me, too. But we have to stay calm. I don't know—"

The creature slapped a tentacle down beside them

with a suddenness that made them both jump. "Where am I?"

Derek was astounded to hear a note of fear in its voice.

"You're on Earth," stammered Jenny. Then she added in a whisper, "I hope."

The creature made a bubbling noise deep in its throat. "The coven! Is the coven trying to come back?"

"What coven?" asked Derek. "What are you talking about?

"Nothing!" said the creature desperately. "Nothing!"

Derek glanced back at Jenny. She was white-faced and shaking with fear. He stepped back to comfort her, but before he could put his arm around her, the creature lashed out with another tentacle. Moving like a whip, it struck the floor just to their right with a *thwack*, splattering slime in all directions. Now a thick tentacle lay undulating on either side of them.

"Don't move," said the creature.

Derek considered trying to grab the broomstick and smash one of the tentacles. He decided against it, fearing he might only succeed in angering the creature. He looked at Jenny. Her lower lip was trembling. He hoped she wasn't going to cry.

A period of tense silence followed while the creature looked them over. Derek had the uneasy feeling they were being judged. Suddenly he found the silence unbearable. To break it, he asked, "Who does the sword belong to?"

"Mormekull," the creature replied. "Sort of."

"The enemy!" gasped Jenny.

Derek wondered how the creature would react to *that* bit of information.

But all it said was, "Well, he's no friend of mine, either. I just work for him." It paused, then asked, "What do *you* want with the sword? And why is Mormekull your enemy?"

"We were playing a game," said Derek. He stopped. It sounded so silly. How could he explain to this . . . *thing* what was going on? Especially since he really had no idea himself.

"We need it to break a spell," he said at last.

"What kind of spell?"

"One of banishment. We want to return home."

"Uh-oh," said the creature. "I don't like the sound of this."

Jenny shivered. Derek was talking to the tentacled beast as if the game was real. Her heart began to pound harder as she realized there was no "as if" about it. The game *was* real. Why else would they be standing here talking to a monster?

Suddenly the creature turned in her direction, a movement accomplished by twisting the lower part of its squat body, which seemed very flexible. "Are you part of the coven?" it asked.

Its voice was so serious Jenny knew she had to answer correctly. She glanced at Derek, hoping for a clue, but he shook his head helplessly. "I don't know," she said finally.

The creature snorted. "That's stupid!"

"No, it's not," said Derek. "Listen. Let me tell you what happened."

Quickly he outlined what had brought them to the cellar. The creature listened, its lopsided eyes blinking every now and then, its tentacles rippling uneasily.

"Take me to the others," it said when he was done.

Derek looked at Jenny. "The others?"

"That's what I said!" snapped the creature. Its voice had a hint of ancient anger and lurking sorrow. "Don't act so surprised. I have some old scores to settle, and you may be able to help."

When neither one of them answered, it wrapped a tentacle around Jenny's waist and lifted her from the floor.

"Take me to the others," it repeated.

Jenny, pale and trembling, looked at Derek with pleading eyes.

"All right," he said firmly. "Let go of her. Then follow me."

9

THE POWERS THAT BE

Denise stood at the top of the stairs, unable to see any way to help Matt, who seemed to have lost his mind. He was backing down the stairway, a look of desperation on his face as he swung some sort of stick ferociously back and forth in front of him.

Niana!

She spun around, but could not see who had spoken.

"Denise!" cried Matt desperately. He was at the foot of the stairs now, still backing up. Suddenly he shouted in pain. Denise gasped as she saw a broad rip appear in the right shoulder of his shirt. Beneath the rip his flesh was torn, too. Blood began pouring down his arm.

Finally understanding that he really was being attacked by something she could not see, Denise hurtled down the stairway, heedless of whatever it was that stood between herself and Matt.

"Be careful!" cried Matt. "They'll get you, too!"

Denise stopped, uncertain what to do.

Tansy leaned over the stair railing. "The stave!" she cried. "Matt, they want the stave!"

"Can you see what's going on?" yelled Denise.

"No, but I can *hear* them. There are two of them, and they want Matt to give them the stave."

"They can't have it!" shouted Matt.

"Tansy, we've got to do something!" cried Denise frantically.

Tansy started down the stairs.

"Be careful, miss!" cried Charity. "Those two with the swords are a rough-looking pair."

"Can *you* see them?" asked Tansy in surprise.

"Of course. Can't you?"

"Who are you talking to?" called Denise, her voice shrill with fear.

Tansy did not answer. Something was bothering her, a thought at the back of her mind struggling to take form. What had triggered it? Charity had been talking . . .

That was it! Denise couldn't hear Charity, but she, Tansy, could! She recalled Travis's first statement of her powers: "You are an enchantress who can communicate with spirits."

Could it be that her game powers were real?

If so, then maybe Matt's powers would be, too.

"Matt!" she cried. "Your spells. *Use your spells!*"

Matt looked up. A light of understanding crossed his face. He swung the stave ferociously, then cast it behind him. With grim concentration he raised his hands.

"Charity," said Tansy. "What are the men doing? Tell me quickly!"

"They're backing off, as if they're expecting something to happen. Why did the boy throw away his stick?"

"Watch," said Tansy.

Suddenly Matt's hands erupted in flame, fire shooting from his fingertips, from his palms—a blaze of blue and yellow heat that engulfed his arms to the elbows.

Denise began to scream.

Tansy grabbed her shoulder. "It's all right," she said. "It's all right. That's his power!"

"Oh, that's done it, miss!" cried Charity triumphantly. "That's done it for sure."

A line of blue fire stretched across the hallway. Matt stood on one side of it, sweat running down his brow. The tip of his tongue protruded from his lips and his face was lined with fierce concentration.

"Look out!" cried Charity. "They're running from him, but they're coming this way. Stand aside!"

Tansy grabbed Denise and pulled her against the banister. The girls shuddered as a cold wind whipped past them.

"Well," said Charity, sounding surprised but satisfied. "They just disappeared. I guess that's that!"

"Matt!" cried Denise. Pulling away from Tansy, she raced down the steps. The line of fire was flickering out now, and Matt had a dazed expression on his face.

He lifted his hands, looked at them as if he had never seen them before, then crumpled and fell to the floor.

Denise was at his side instantly. Kneeling, she shook his shoulder. "Matt! *Matt!*"

"The fire, miss," said Charity nervously.

Tansy turned her attention from her friends and saw that though the magical flames had gone out, several spots in the hallway had caught fire for real and were beginning to blaze away.

She looked at Matt. He could cast spells of fire and illusion. She had a spell for fire, too. A spell for fire, and a spell for freezing.

She walked slowly down the steps. How had Matt done it?

Raising her hands, Tansy pointed them at the closest patch of flames. She began to concentrate, imagining a blast of cold so intense it could kill the fire.

Ice. Ice and snow. Freezing.

Suddenly she felt as if she had been plunged into a vat of ice water. A ring of cold around her heart threatened to stop it from beating. Then a burst of frost surged out of her fingertips, struck the nearest patch of fire, and extinguished it instantly.

There remained three spots where the fire was a serious problem. Setting her feet slightly apart to brace herself, Tansy directed a blast of frost at each of them.

At once the flames were gone.

"Oh, that was wonderful, miss!" cried Charity.

"It hurts," gasped Tansy. Groaning with pain at the intense cold, she wondered if Matt had experienced heat in the same extreme. If so, it was little wonder he had collapsed. She put her hand to her forehead. She didn't feel very well.

"Oh, miss!" cried Charity as Tansy crumpled and fell to the floor.

Travis sat at the table, waiting for the others to return. He flipped through the game manual impatiently. Sending them all through the house had been a good idea, except for one thing: It left *him* sitting here along, doing nothing.

He put the book down and smiled. At least it would be fun when they came back. He couldn't wait to hear what they would have to say. That plastic octopus of his little sister's that he had put in the cellar should have been just enough to give Jenny a bit of a scare without getting her too upset. And the tape recorder in the attic had probably given Tansy a good jump, too. But she wouldn't mind, not really. She'd be a little angry at first, but she could take it. That was one of the things he liked about her.

He heard a noise in the hall and looked up. Some of the searchers were on their way back. He started to stand, then thought better of it. Let them think he had been waiting casually while they finished their assignments.

He turned back to the game book. He needed to brush up on the next stage of the game anyway. But the sound of the rain slashing at the windows behind him was distracting, and the flickering candlelight made reading difficult. Most of all, his eagerness for the others to return made concentration almost impossible.

He put his finger on the page, as if he could force his attention to stay with the material by touching the printed words.

"Once the objects of power have been regathered, the Master Mage must take a more active hand. There is apt to be conflict among the players about how to use the items. Master Mage Karno must negotiate . . ."

Travis looked up again. The noise in the hall was louder this time.

He frowned. Had the others decided to get back at him for his little tricks? He pulled back his chair, stood, and listened carefully. He could hear Tansy's voice.

Why was she yelling?

He started for the door, then stopped in his tracks.

Someone was in the room with him.

He turned around to see if one of the others had snuck in somehow.

The room was empty.

But it wasn't! There *was* someone else. He knew it as surely as he knew his own name. He could feel it—feel the presence of another being.

Travis.

The voice was rich and deep.

Travis began to tremble. Outside there was a horrible crash of thunder. He turned to face the table, then cried out in fear.

Slowly, one by one, the candles were going out.

When Denise saw Tansy fall, she scrambled to her feet. She looked at Tansy, then at Matt.

She had to get them to the library. It wasn't that

far—she could just go for help. But considering everything that had happened already, she didn't want to leave them alone for even a moment. Who knew what might happen while she went to get Travis?

She took a deep breath. The one thing she understood about the bizarre scene that had just occurred was that Tansy and Matt had been using their game powers. Was it possible hers worked, too?

Furrowing her brow in concentration, Denise passed her hands over Matt's body.

Even though it was what she was *trying* to do, she gasped when his body slowly lifted from the floor and rose until it was floating about three feet in the air.

Once she had Tansy floating, too, she turned and headed for the library.

10

MAGIC TAKES OVER

"No!" cried Travis.

The room grew darker.

Travis, said the voice. *You* can *be the Master Mage. We can give you power—the kind of power you've always dreamed of. No one will ever laugh at you again. Nothing will be impossible for you. All you need to do is let me in.*

Travis clapped his hands to the sides of his head. The voice was already inside. He remembered Lydia's screams the night they had first tried to play the game, and what she had said to Tansy later about "fingers" in her mind. Now he knew what those strange words meant. Someone was trying to get inside *his* brain. The attack came as a strange probing feeling that made him squirm with disgust.

"Stop it!" he cried.

Just then the library door swung open. Travis staggered back against the table as he saw first Matt and then Tansy float through the doorway. They were lying on their backs, about three feet above the floor. The stave lay on Matt's chest.

Denise appeared in the doorway, hands held out before her, face dripping with perspiration. With a sigh she lowered her hands. Matt and Tansy settled to the floor, dropping as lightly as balloons that were slowly losing their helium.

Once they were safely down, Denise sagged against the doorsill with a little moan of exhaustion.

Travis looked from Matt and Tansy to Denise and back again. Suddenly he realized that the fingers in his mind were gone.

Tansy moaned and turned on her side.

Travis licked his lips. His throat was dry. When he tried to speak, nothing came out. He swallowed, tried again. "Denise, what's going on?"

"That's what I wanted to ask you," she replied, and Travis found the haunted look in her eyes as frightening as anything that had happened in the last few minutes. He had never seen the unshakable Denise look this way. A pang of helpless terror shot through him.

"What . . . what happened to Matt and Tansy?" he stammered.

"They wore themselves out. Using their spells."

Travis looked at her incredulously. "What . . ."

Tansy moaned again, and then opened her eyes. "Travis?"

He rushed to her, knelt at her side. "Tansy! Are you all right?"

She put her hand to her forehead. "I . . . I think so. Matt! Matt, are you . . ." Her voice trailed off as she realized that Matt could not answer her.

Denise had crossed to join them. Kneeling, she lifted Matt's head into her lap. "Matt," she whispered. "Matty, it's me, Denise. Matt, wake up!"

As she stroked his forehead, his eyes flickered open.

Travis shivered. "Your name is Niana," he whispered. "You are a healer."

Denise glared at him. "Don't call me that!"

Travis stepped back, startled by the intensity of her anger.

"They want me," said Denise. Her eyes were large, her voice desperate. "They want me to *be* Niana. Don't help them!"

Matt moaned and sat up. "Denise? What happened? The warriors . . ."

"Oh, he's awake, miss. I'm glad. I was so worried."

"Charity?" asked Tansy. "Where are you?"

"Right here, miss. Standing beside you."

Travis and Denise glanced at each other, then stared nervously at Tansy, wondering who she was talking to—or if she had simply lost her mind. But Matt leaped to his feet and cried out in terror, "Tansy! Tansy, there's someone beside you!"

"You can see her?" asked Tansy in surprise. "Oh, of course you can. That's your power! It's all right, Matt. She's a friend."

"What the hell are you two talking about?" asked Travis.

Matt was holding on to the back of a chair for support. "There's someone standing beside Tansy," he said. "A girl. A ghost! Can't you see her? Denise? Travis?"

Denise shook her head. Travis rubbed his eyes and stared at Tansy.

"Of course they can't see her," said Tansy. "They don't have the power. Remember the game, Matt. You're the only one who was given the power to see spirits."

"Do you want me to go, miss?" asked Charity, a note of sadness in her voice. "I don't want to cause trouble."

"No," said Tansy. "We'll get things straightened out in a minute. Travis, why don't you light the rest of the candles? It's dark in here."

His long fingers trembling, Travis took out a pack of matches and fumbled with the candles, glad to have something to do.

"Let's sit," said Tansy. "I think we need to calm down and talk this whole thing over. Matt, this is Charity. She's on our side."

"Charity?" asked Travis. The color drained from his face. "Not the murdered maid?"

"That's me," said Charity, with a hint of pride.

"They can't hear you, Charity," said Tansy. "I'm the only one you can speak to." She turned to Matt and asked, "What does she look like?"

"She's very pretty," said Matt shakily. "At least, as far as I can make out. She's there, but she's not there, if you know what I mean. I can see right through her.

She's wearing a nightgown—an old-fashioned one. And she has a ribbon around her neck."

"That's how I was dressed when it happened," said Charity significantly.

"She has curly hair. I think it's blond, but I'm not certain. Now she's smiling at me." Matt found himself smiling back, in spite of himself. "She's got a very pretty smile."

"Thank you," said Charity.

"Don't you think you should let the rest of us in on this?" snapped Travis.

"Haven't you figured it out yet?" asked Tansy. "The game is coming true!"

"The game is coming true," repeated Travis, as if the words had no meaning.

"Either that," said Denise, "or we're all losing our minds . . . or sharing the same nightmare." Tansy could hear a touch of hysteria in her voice. "I suppose that makes as much sense as anything else."

Now it was out in the open. There was a moment of awkward silence.

"Well, the *first* thing," said Matt at last, "is to find out what's happened to Derek and Jenny."

"We're all right," said Derek, stepping through the door. Jenny was clinging to his arm. They looked nervous. "But we've got a little . . . surprise for you." He looked around the table where his four friends were sitting. "What's going on here, anyway? You four look as though you'd just seen a ghost."

"Just one of us has," said Matt.

"Maybe they won't be as shocked as we thought," said Jenny.

"Shocked at what?" asked Denise. Suddenly she realized what Derek was holding. "You've got the sword!"

Derek smiled. "We sure do. It's a beaut, isn't it?"

Travis's face had gone dead white. "Where did you get that?" he asked softly.

"From the cellar," said Derek. "Where you put it."

"But it's not the one I put there. I never saw it before."

"Figures," snorted Derek. "Look, you guys, there is something very weird going on here."

"We know," said Matt.

"Well, even so, you'd better brace yourselves for this one." Derek drew Jenny to his side.

The others stared in their direction. Suddenly Travis leaped to his feet, bumping the table so hard the candles almost fell over. Denise let out a gasp. Charity began to scream.

Looming in the doorway was the Guardian of the Sword. Tentacles dripping, it slithered into the room. It turned its baleful glare from face to face, then said, "We have to talk."

11

TRAPPED!

The room exploded in a hurricane of movement and shouting. Then, just as suddenly, there was silence. Matt, Denise, Travis, and Tansy stood pressed against the walls, as far from the monster as they could get. Gasping for breath, they looked desperately at the door, which was blocked by the creature's bulk.

"Are you through panicking?" asked Derek, a hint of smugness in his voice.

Travis swallowed hard. "Derek, what is that thing?"

The creature lifted itself on its tentacles, which brought its head close to the ceiling. Looking down at the players, it said in a strangely dignified voice, "I am not a *thing*. I am the Guardian of the Sword. And while I do not know who you are, either, I do know this much: You are in big trouble. If you are lucky, I may be able to help you."

"Help us?" asked Matt. "How do we know you won't just kill us?"

The creature extended a tentacle and laid it across Matt's shoulder. Matt shuddered, but held his ground.

Its voice soft and oily, the creature said, "I could have killed Derek and Jenny in the cellar, had I wanted. I could have killed them, then come after the rest of you, silently strangling you one by one. . . ."

As it spoke it extended the tentacle, wrapping it around Matt's neck like some huge, glistening earthworm. All at once it pulled tight. Matt's eyes bulged. He clawed at his throat.

"You see?" said the creature, ignoring Matt's fingers. "It would have been simple. But I chose not to, because I think we can help one another."

It retracted its tentacle, leaving Matt rubbing his neck in disgust.

The confusion broke out anew. It was Travis, suddenly resuming his position as leader of the group, who quieted things by the simple expedient of bellowing, "STOP IT!"

The room fell silent. He looked at his friends one by one, then said, "I think we should listen to him."

"Wait a minute," said Tansy. "Matt, where's Charity? I haven't heard her since . . . since . . ." She gestured at the creature, uncertain how to finish her sentence.

Matt looked around. "She's lying on the floor! Good grief, I think she fainted. Wait a minute. She's sitting up. But she's white as a . . ." His voice trailed off.

"It's all right, miss," said Charity, in a voice that only Tansy could hear. "I just took a bit of a fright. But what is that thing?"

"I'm not sure," said Tansy quietly. She felt strange talking to Charity in front of the others.

"Why don't you all take a seat," said the creature.

Slowly, cautiously, the players took their places around the library table. Then they watched uneasily as the Guardian of the Sword used its tentacles to move itself to a chair at the end of the table.

A trail of slime marked where it had passed.

Using four tentacles to pull itself up, and two more to brace itself, it settled into the chair with a sigh, its shiny body lapping over in all directions.

Charity, now hovering at Tansy's elbow, whispered in her ear, "I don't like this, miss. I don't like it at all."

"Shhh! We need to listen."

"All right, O Mighty Master Mage," said Derek. "Suppose you tell us what's going on?"

"What did you call him?" asked the creature sharply.

"Master Mage," said Derek. "It's his role in the game."

An angry look came into the creature's eyes. Tansy shivered. She expected it to speak, but it remained silent.

"I don't *know* what's going on," said Travis, glancing at the creature nervously. "Maybe we should start by telling each other what's been happening. That might help us make some sense out of this."

"I have a better idea," said Jenny. "Why don't we just get out of here?"

The players looked at one another hesitantly, reluctant to put their fear into words.

"Come on," said Jenny. "What are you waiting for?"

It was Tansy who finally spoke. "If the game is really coming true—"

"Then the house is sealed, and we won't be able to leave," finished Denise, her voice husky with fear.

"Oh," said Jenny softly.

"The first thing we should do is check that out," said Travis. He looked around the table. "Derek, Matt . . ."

"No," said Tansy. "All of us."

Travis nodded. "All right—let's go."

Grimly the group stood and left the room. As they walked down the hallway, Tansy kept telling herself that they would simply go down to the main floor, open the door, and leave. They'd get a little wet in the storm, but other than that nothing would happen.

They descended the stairs in wary silence, traveling two by two, with the creature bringing up the rear.

When they reached the foyer, Travis went to the door.

It wouldn't open.

After rattling the knob several times, Travis turned to Jenny. "Maybe you'd better try."

"Me?" she asked, looking puzzled.

"Well, you do have spells for opening locks."

She blinked in surprise, then nodded. But nothing she could do would cause the door to open, either.

"Probably the spell that sealed the house is stronger than the spells she was given to deal with locks," said Denise.

"Well, one of *my* powers is extraordinary strength," said Derek. With that, he hurled himself at the door. It actually bulged outward—then snapped back, flinging him across the room.

Tansy could feel a palpable fear rising in her chest. This was getting weirder by the second. "Are there any other doors?" she asked, her voice little more than a husky whisper.

"One in the kitchen, and one that leads out from the cellar," Travis replied.

"Let's go," said Matt.

Derek and Jenny led the way, retracing their earlier path.

To no one's surprise, the kitchen door was sealed as firmly as the one in the foyer.

They all eyed the cellar door nervously. It was their last chance.

"Well, here goes," whispered Travis. A shout of joy went up when he turned the knob and the door swung open.

Their exultation quickly turned to terror.

On the other side of the door was not the cellar, but a vast cavern. Shining their flashlights into it, they saw stalagmites and stalactites, strange rock formations, and something gray and shiny that looked like a giant fungus. In the distance they could hear a river.

Jenny began to cry.

"Home!" cried the creature.

Tansy jumped. She had almost forgotten it was with them.

"That's fine for you," said Derek. "But it doesn't help the rest of us much."

The creature made a scornful sound. "And if that had been a way out for you, were you planning to stay and help *me* find a way home?" it asked.

Tansy felt a twinge of guilt.

"I thought not," said the creature, when no one spoke. "However, unlike you, I have every intention of seeing this thing through. Home can wait. It's not much of a home anyway—though as much of one as I am ever likely to have now. But as I told you, I have some old scores to settle."

It was a much subdued group that gathered back in the library. Fear seemed to have drained their energy. Derek and Jenny stood by the door. Jenny, clinging to Derek, was weeping quietly. Noting that several of the candles had again gone out, Denise began to relight them. Travis and Tansy were whispering together, while Charity stood beside them, listening intently. The creature squatted in the center of the room, plucking books from the shelves with its tentacles and leafing through the pages as if it might find some answer in there.

Outside, the storm continued to rage.

"This is crazy!" cried Matt. He was pacing back and forth by the windows. "We're just sitting here like a bunch of idiots. There has to be a way out!" He looked at the others. Tansy shivered.

The desperation in Matt's eyes was growing. Suddenly he picked up a chair. With a cry of rage he swung it against a window.

The chair flew into a hundred little pieces.

The glass was unbroken.

Matt slumped to the floor, staring at his hands as if they had been burned. Denise rushed to his side. "Did you hurt yourself?" she cried.

He shook his head, mute and hopeless. Suddenly tears began to stream down his face.

Denise put her arm around him, held his face against her shoulder. "Travis," she said. *"Do something."*

"Me?" Travis looked around the room, bewildered. The others were all staring at him, even the creature.

"I can't . . . I'm not . . ."

He trailed off into a long moment of silence. Watching his face, Tansy could sense the struggle going on inside him. She knew he was terrified. But she also knew that if any of them could find an answer, it was Travis. She laid her hand on his, squeezed it reassuringly.

And once again, though the game had gone beyond his control, he was the leader. He gave her a gentle smile. "The answer is obvious. *We have to win the game!* Find the objects, complete the spell, and we're out of the house. Come on! We don't have much time."

It was as if they had been given an extension on a death warrant. Lifted by his energy, the others collected around the table.

"We've already got the sword and the stave," said Travis.

"Right," said Derek. He placed the objects on the table where everyone could see them. There was a murmur of appreciation for the sword, which sparkled in the candlelight. Next to it lay the stave that Matt had managed to save from the two warriors. The wood was dark and polished, with an intricate grain.

Tansy reached out and placed a tentative finger against it, then drew her hand back in shock. "It feels . . . alive," she said. "Like there's electricity going through it or something."

One by one the others touched the stave and muttered their agreement.

"All right," said Travis. "The first thing we have to do is find the rod and the ring. Tansy, it was your job to seek the ring."

She nodded. "I was looking for it in the attic."

Travis smiled. "You were on the right track. At least, you were before all this started. Assuming it's still where I left it—or that whatever has replaced it is there—you can just go back up and get it. You'll find it—"

Suddenly Travis looked oddly uncomfortable. He put his hands to his throat, as if he was choking. His eyes bulged, and though he moved his mouth, no sound came out.

12

DOUBLE DISCOVERY

"What's wrong?" asked Tansy. "Travis, are you all right?"

"It's the spell!" said Denise. "Remember? One of the rules of the game was that he couldn't tell us where anything is."

"Are you all right?" cried Tansy again.

Travis nodded. His eyes had begun to water, and he wiped at them. "I think so," he gasped. He cleared his throat two or three times.

"You're sure not going to be much help," said Derek in disgust.

"I may not be much," snapped Travis, "but I'm all you've got. You're just going to have to use your new powers a little more efficiently. Your brains, too."

"Do you suppose you can still answer questions?" asked Jenny timidly.

"It would make sense," said Travis, "since that's my function in the game. Ask me something."

"Where's the ring?" asked Tansy.

He shook his head. "That won't do any good. Even if you ask me directly, I can't tell you flat-out. You've got to go for clues."

"It seemed worth a try," said Tansy defensively. She sat back and waited for someone else to ask a question.

"You'd better *keep* trying, Tansy," said Denise. "You're the only one who's been in the attic."

Tansy frowned. She tried to think of how she would phrase the question if they were playing Spirits and Spells for fun.

"I'm in the attic," she said. "I have defeated—sort of—the spirit that guards the place. Is there a treasure in this room?"

"Yes," said Travis.

"Are there any clues to its location?"

After a moment Travis said, "Yes.

"The treasure is a golden ring
Suited for a banished king.
Search for it where smoke is rising;
What you find may be surprising."

He blinked, then shook his head as if coming out of a trance.

Tansy smiled. "I've got it!" Her smile faded. "Only who's actually going to go get it?"

"Let's all go together," said Jenny.

"I don't think we have time," said Matt. "It might make more sense to split into two groups. That way we don't have to go alone, but we can get the stuff we need to get out of here faster."

"Well, I might as well go back to the attic," said Tansy, "since I already know my way around there. And Charity can help me. Matt, why don't you come with us? Since you can see her and I can hear her, the three of us ought to be able to work together."

Travis's face darkened at this suggestion, but he said nothing.

"Assuming we need to stick as close to the game as possible, then I have to be the one to go look for the rod," said Denise. "If Matt is going with Tansy, then maybe Derek and Jenny can come with me."

"I think I should accompany you as well," said the Guardian of the Sword.

"Maybe you should stay in the library and guard the things we already have," suggested Derek.

"I think I have to do that," said Travis. "It's my role in the game. Besides, you're more apt to need his help than I am. Just get going and get back here with those things as fast as you can. I'll study the game book to see if I can figure out what to do next."

Despite his brave words, Travis felt scared and lonely as he watched his friends head down the hallway. Though his excuses for not going with them, for being the one to stay in the library, had made sense, they weren't the real reason he had suggested they go without him.

In fact, he wasn't sure of the real reason. When he thought about it, he was pretty sure that, if anything, having the two objects of power here would make the library a focal point for attacks. And if the guardians of the rod and the stave were any indication, he'd need all the help he could get if that happened.

Yet *something* had prompted him to send the others away.

Now, standing at the door, he wanted to cry out to them, beg them to stay—or to take him along. But he couldn't seem to make the words come out. Mute and terrified, he watched as the last tentacle disappeared up the hallway.

He was alone.

No. He wasn't. His scalp began to tingle and once again he had the distinct impression that someone was nearby. Turning to look in the other direction, he tightened his grip on the doorknob and tried to hold back a scream.

Four creatures stood at the head of the main stairwell. Short and squat, they had faces with piglike snouts and gleaming yellow tusks. They were dressed in leather armor and carrying short swords and round shields.

"Goblins!" whispered Travis in horror.

The creatures glanced about, as if trying to decide where to go. Suddenly they spotted him and started in his direction. Travis stepped back quickly, ready to slam the library door shut and brace himself against it. But as the goblins drew closer, he saw that they were oddly translucent, the way he had imagined a ghost would look. They were here, and yet not here.

He decided that, transparent or not, he didn't want to face them. He closed the door and braced himself against it, then decided that was inadequate. Fearful something might try to enter before he had a chance to secure the door, he raced to the table and shot back with a chair, which he propped under the doorknob.

He waited, expecting to hear goblin swords beating against the door at any second.

The only sound that came to him was the rain beating against the windows.

Had the goblins gone past? He wanted to open the door and see. But what if they were waiting in silence to trap him? Perhaps the moment he opened the door, they would come leaping through and slash him to bits with their swords.

He pressed his ear against the wood.

Nothing.

Could they be gone?

You have nothing to fear, said a voice, the same voice he had heard before. *You are the Master Mage. Let me in—I will protect you.*

Travis looked around wildly. "Where are you? Who are you?"

I am Karno! Let me in.

"No!" cried Travis. "No! No! No!"

Falling to his knees, he clutched at his temples, trying to hold out the icy fingers prying at his mind.

Tansy, Matt, and Charity stood at the entrance to the attic. Matt could see that Charity was speaking, but he couldn't hear a word of what she was saying.

"What was that all about?" he asked when Charity's lips stopped moving.

"She said there's something here," replied Tansy. "Something that doesn't belong here."

"Great. Did she tell you what it is?"

"No. But she says she's scared."

"She's scared? What about us?"

Tansy clapped her hand across his mouth to silence him.

"What's she scared of?" asked Matt in a whisper after Tansy had removed her fingers from his lips. "They can't hurt her—she's already dead."

Tansy bent her head to listen to Charity, then repeated her words to Matt: "The torments of the soul are worse than those of the body."

He snorted. "Sounds like a sermon."

"Charity says she wouldn't know about that," said Tansy after a moment. "She was a wicked girl and almost never went to church."

"For Pete's sake," said Matt. "We don't have time for this. Let's find that ring and get out of here! Where did you decide it was? You sure perked up when Travis gave you that last clue."

Tansy smiled. "As soon as he said, 'Search for it where smoke is rising,' I knew I had it. There's a big chimney at the other end of the attic. It's got to be hidden there."

"I never liked it down there," said Charity. "It always made me uneasy."

"What's bothering her now?" asked Matt. "She looks scared."

Tansy repeated what Charity had said.

Matt took Tansy's hand. She understood that the gesture had nothing to do with romance. "Well, come on. The sooner we find that thing, the sooner we can get out of here."

They entered the attic and began walking rapidly along the aisle, ignoring the clutter on either side. Suddenly a rat scuttled across the floor in front of them. Its eyes glowed red in the beam of Tansy's flashlight. Even worse, its body was easily two feet long, larger than a big cat's. Tansy and Matt stopped so abruptly that they nearly knocked each other over.

"We never had rats here before!" screamed Charity as the creature disappeared behind a broken-down armchair.

Matt and Tansy stared after it, neither of them willing to move until they were sure it wasn't coming back. Finally Matt swallowed uncomfortably and said, "Well, we've killed plenty of giant rats in our gaming careers. I guess we can handle one or two more, if we have to."

Swinging his flashlight around the piles of stuff nearest them, he located a broken kitchen chair. He handed Tansy the flashlight, then wrenched the chair apart. Keeping one of the legs for himself, he traded another to Tansy for his flashlight. Face grim, he said, "These will do for weapons, until we can find something better."

They moved forward again, shining their lights in all directions.

After a moment Tansy said, "Did you notice that the rat seemed a little . . ." She fumbled for an appropriate word. "A little *dim?*"

"I never saw a rat that looked real intelligent."

She made a sound of exasperation. "No. Like it was fading out or something."

Matt thought for a moment, then said, "If the house is overlapping with some other reality, maybe the rat wasn't really here. Or we're not really where it is. Or something. Geez, Tansy, I don't know what the hell is going on."

They heard another scuttling, and two more rats darted in front of them. Charity let out a little shriek. Matt and Tansy moved closer together.

The rats did not seem to notice them.

They waited until the rats were out of sight, then moved forward again.

"Well, this is it," said Tansy when they stood facing the large stone chimney a moment later. "Let's start looking."

The mortar around several of the stones appeared loose, and Tansy had the feeling that perhaps Travis had hidden the ring behind one of them.

Lightning flickered outside, and Tansy crossed to peer out one of the windows. At first she could see nothing. But when the lightning flickered again, she cried in horror. "Matt! Look!"

Matt glanced out the other window as the lightning flickered a third time. "So what was I supposed to see?" he asked, after the darkness returned. "It's a nice view, but we don't have time—"

"You didn't see anything strange?" demanded Tansy.

"No. Just a lawn and shrubs and—"

"Come here. Look out this window."

Matt crossed to stand beside her. It was very dark outside, and at first all he could see was droplets of rain spattering against the window, making trails down the glass. Then there was another flash of lightning.

It was Matt's turn to cry out in shock. What he had seen out the first window was the backyard of the Gulbrandsen estate. Through this window he saw something else altogether—a strange, rocky landscape cut with gorges and ravines, dotted with sparse, straggling trees, and pocked with oily pools. A misshapen creature slouched away from one of the pools, heading in the general direction of the house.

"Let's find that ring and get out of here," said Matt after a brief silence. "Now!"

Tansy began poking at one of the stones that looked loose. Matt took out his pocketknife and prodded at the mortar, trying to find a crumbly patch that might indicate a hidden compartment.

Suddenly he looked up. "Did you hear that?" he asked nervously.

"Hear what?"

"I thought I heard someone call my name."

"Ignore it!" said Tansy. "Shut it out of your head! And keep looking."

Matt continued to work away at the mortar. Twice more he glanced up, disturbed. But he said nothing.

"I think I see a loose one, miss," said Charity. "It's up pretty high. You'll need a chair to reach it."

"Show Matt," said Tansy. "Matt, watch Charity. She's going to point out a likely stone to you."

Matt looked up. He nodded, then dragged an old chair out of a pile of debris. He stood on it and began to work at a stone some seven feet from the floor. Tansy continued to work at stones closer to the bottom of the chimney.

Suddenly they both cried out in triumph, "I think I've got it!"

Confused, they glanced at each other, then continued to work at the loose stones they had found.

Matt managed to free his first. After pulling it from the chimney, he reached into the space behind it.

"Bingo!" he crowed as he extracted a large golden ring.

It was not a finger ring, as he had expected, but a band made to fit around a person's arm. It appeared to be made of solid gold. Set in ornate patterns on its surface were several dozen emeralds and rubies.

Before Matt could show Tansy his find, she succeeded in prying loose a much larger stone from near the base of the chimney. The stone fell to the floor with a crash, followed by a tinkling clatter.

With a cry of horror, she jumped back.

13

INTO THE CLOSET

Derek switched on his flashlight. "So you think the rod is in one of the bedrooms up there?" he said to Denise.

She nodded. "The first clue said something about 'sleeping power.' I think it was a pun. And this time Travis said, 'Seek it in the Master room, Where the Master met his doom,' which I figure has to mean the master bedroom. One of the Gulbrandsens must have died in bed or something."

"We should have asked Travis if it was guarded," said Jenny as they reached the top of the stairs.

"I don't think that would have done any good," said the creature. "He doesn't know what's going on now any more than we do. The whole thing is out of his control."

Denise looked uneasy. "Speaking of guarded . . . did either of you hear anything funny when you were searching before?"

"No," said Jenny. "Why?"

Denise looked away for a second, then said, "I thought I heard someone calling my name—my name for the game. I didn't like it."

"Maybe it was your imagination," said Derek.

Denise snorted. "If it was, that would make it the only imaginary thing that's happened so far tonight."

"I guess you're right," said Derek. "But maybe that part is over." He pointed the flashlight down the hallway. "Any idea which of these is the master bedroom?"

Denise shrugged. "No. I had only got through about half of them when I heard Matt yelling. And I wasn't looking for a master bedroom then, just another clue of some kind."

"Let's pick up where you left off," suggested Jenny.

With Denise in the lead, the three teens and the monster walked down the hall. All were uneasily aware that there might be something lurking behind any door, waiting to leap out and attack them.

The first three rooms they tried were obviously wrong. They were pleasant, or would be in the daytime, and once they were cleaned and scrubbed. But each was too small for a master bedroom.

"Look at this," said Denise as they crossed the hall to try a fourth door. "It's a long way to the next door—which could mean this is a big room. Maybe it's the one."

"Allow me," said the creature. It slithered a tentacle past the three searchers and deftly twisted the doorknob.

The door swung open with a creak. Jenny rubbed her arms, trying to smooth down the goose bumps.

Derek stepped in and swung his flashlight around the room. "Looks good," he said. "It's still furnished."

The others crowded in behind him.

"Look at that bed!" said Denise. "This has got to be it."

The bed was a huge four-poster, covered by a dark, tattered canopy.

"I bet it's someplace around that," said Jenny. "Let's look!"

Staying close together, they crossed the room. Denise got down on her hands and knees to search under the bed. Derek and Jenny looked on either side.

"Do you suppose it might be in that closet?" Jenny asked, gesturing to a door on her side of the bed.

"We'll check there next," said Derek.

The creature had extended two tentacles to the top of the canopy. Contracting them, it pulled itself up so it could peer over the ruffles. "Nothing up here," it said. "Except dust." It began to choke. "Faugh! All this dryness is bad for my skin!"

"Nothing down here, either," said Denise at last. Climbing to her feet, she added, "Looks like we've struck out."

"Try the closet, Jenny," said Derek.

"Wait!" cried Denise.

The warning came too late; Jenny had already begun to open the door. As she did, their flashlights died, all three of them going out simultaneously.

Voices rose in panic as the room was plunged into total darkness. Jenny's scream cut above them. "Derek! Derek, it's got me!"

"What's got you?" cried Derek. "Jenny, what is it?"

A flash of lightning illumined a sight that made Denise cry out in horror. An emaciated arm, robed in black, had reached out of the closet and grabbed Jenny by the hand. Now it was trying to pull her through the doorway, back into the closet. She was struggling fiercely, her feet braced against the doorsill, her free hand clutching the woodwork.

As quickly as it had come, the lightning was gone, and the darkness returned.

"DEREK!"

Jenny's scream reverberated through the darkened room.

Derek leaped across the bed. "Jenny! Jenny, hang on!"

The closet door slammed shut.

The screaming stopped.

Jenny was gone.

Travis poked his head out of the room, then stepped into the hallway. Looking furtively to the right and then the left, he walked slowly back to the library.

A misty-looking ogre went strolling past him, a club over one shoulder, its knuckles dragging on the floor.

Travis ignored it.

He entered the library, sat down at the table, and closed his eyes. A moment later he shook his head and opened them again, wondering what had happened.

"Boy, I don't know how I can be sleepy with all

this going on," he said, stretching and giving a hearty yawn. "It must be really late."

He turned back to the game book, trying to figure out what to do when the others got back.

The shadowy, black-robed figure floating behind him rubbed its hands and smiled with satisfaction.

With his foot braced against the wall, Derek tried to wrench open the closet door. When that failed, he threw himself against it, trying to batter it down.

"Jenny!" he cried. "Jenny, can you hear me?"

He flung himself against the door again and again, screaming her name.

The door was solid as an ancient oak.

No sound came from the other side.

Finally Derek collapsed against the door and began to sob.

A tentacle wrapped itself about his waist and dragged him away from the door. "Let me try," said the creature.

Denise put her arm around Derek. Together they watched as the creature wrapped a long tentacle around the doorknob. Then it stretched two other tentacles toward the bed, coiled them around the posts, and began to pull.

The bed slid across the floor.

"No good," grunted the creature.

It twisted around, looking for something else to grab as an anchor. The room contained nothing heavy enough.

Turning back to the door, the creature slapped one tentacle after another against the wood. Carefully it wriggled the tips into the crack between the door and the frame. Contracting the tentacles, it lifted its whole body from the floor, then pressed itself against the door. It slapped three tentacles out to either side.

They heard a slurping noise, and Derek could see that the creature was pulling against the door with its whole body, which seemed to function like a gigantic suction cup. "Come on!" he cried. "Come on! You can do it!"

The creature's body was expanding and contracting like the throat of a gigantic toad. Throbbing veins rose up all across its back. A low groan issued from its throat.

Still the door wouldn't open.

Finally the wall itself began to crumble. As great chunks of plaster pulled away, the creature lost its hold and tumbled to the floor. Two of its tentacles still extended to the top of the door, it lay gasping and choking, its body trembling with exhaustion.

"No use," it gasped at last. "The door is sealed by magic."

A pained silence settled over them. Derek stared at the floor.

"Denise," said the creature after a moment. "Would you help me? I'm stuck."

When Denise realized what the creature meant, she said, "Oh, sure. Derek, give me a hand."

"What?"

"I said give me a hand. Its tentacles are stuck."

Numbly Derek crossed to the door and bent down. Cupping his hands in front of him, he gave Denise a boost up.

The tentacle was disgusting. She had seen a dead rat once, beside a gutter. It was wet and soggy looking. For some reason the tentacle reminded her of that. It was the same thickness, and when she closed her hand about it, it felt just as she had always imagined the rat would have if she had picked it up. She flinched back.

"Please," said the creature softly. "I'm in pain."

Denise nodded. Setting her jaw, she grabbed the tentacle firmly in one hand. Pulling it away from the door, she was amazed at how the creature had been able to stretch and thin it in order to insert it over the top. With her other hand, she pinched the flesh just outside the wood.

"Ow!"

"I'm sorry. But I can't see any other way to get you loose!"

"It's all right. Go ahead."

She pulled.

Nothing happened. The tentacle was stuck tight.

She pulled again, harder. The tentacle stretched and thinned even more. The glow of the flashlight showed right through the flesh.

What would happen if the tentacle broke?

"Keep trying!" cried the creature.

Pinching tighter, in the desperate hope that it might somehow help keep the tentacle from breaking, she gave a last yank. The tentacle pulled free from the door. She dropped it, and it fell to the floor with a splatting sound.

"Thank you," sighed the creature. "Now the other one."

Denise repeated the process, then leaped down.

"Now," said the creature, "we have to figure out what to do about your friend."

Derek looked at him with sudden hope. "Do you really think—" He was interrupted by the closet door swinging open. "Jenny!" he cried joyfully.

She stepped out of the closet, holding a polished wooden rod that was capped by a ball of smoky crystal. Lights played inside the crystal, dancing across its surface.

Jenny herself was stern and erect, looking at her friends as if she were a queen and they mere commoners.

"Jenny?" asked Derek, his voice now puzzled, worried.

She turned toward him.

"My name," she said, her voice and her eyes as cold as ice, "is Gwynhafra."

14

RATS

"My bones!" cried Charity. "Oh, miss, you found my bones! How clever you are!"

"Clever," said Tansy weakly as she stared in horror at the pieces of smoke-darkened skeleton that had come clattering out of the chimney.

Matt still stood on the chair, clutching the golden arm band and staring down at them in astonishment.

"But it's not happening," moaned Charity. "Oh, it's not working!"

She began to sob.

"What's wrong?" asked Tansy. *"What's* not working?"

"I thought that once I found my bones, I would just fade away," sniffed Charity. "But it's not working. I'm still here! I'm trapped for all eternity!" She let out a screech that made Tansy wonder if her family had mingled with some banshee back in the Old Country.

"Perhaps they just need to be buried," said Tansy sympathetically.

Charity gasped. "You must be right! Will you bury them for me, miss?"

"If we ever get out of this place, I'll be glad to," said Tansy. She turned to Matt. "Help me gather up these bones."

"What?"

"We've got to bury them."

"Tansy . . ."

"Matt, just get a box or something and be quiet, will you? She found where the ring was, didn't she? The least we can do is help her out."

Matt sighed and rummaged in the piles against the wall until he found a suitable box. He dumped the contents without looking at them and returned to Tansy. "Here you go."

"Help me put in the bones," she replied.

He started to protest. But when she knelt and began scooping the old bones into the box, he simply sighed and joined her.

Tansy shuddered when she picked up the first handful. They were smooth and ivory-colored, and she couldn't help but think that they had once been inside a living person; inside Charity. It felt disrespectful to be grabbing them so helter-skelter. But they had no time for ceremony. She was gathering some smaller bones—finger bones, she was pretty sure—when she stopped and clutched Matt's arm. "Did you hear that?"

"What? Did Charity say something? You know I can't—"

Tansy cut him off impatiently. "No, it wasn't Charity. It was a different voice, more like—"

She broke off and looked past him into the darkness. The voice was calling again. It seemed to come from someplace far away, and to be in desperate need.

Tansy, it called. *Tansy, let me come back. It's been so long. Let me come back!* There was a pause. Then the voice said, *Theoni. Let me in. Please.*

"I can hear it, miss!" cried Charity. "It's someone calling your name. And then she called you Theoni."

"That's my name in the . . . in the game," said Tansy. "Come on, Matt. Let's hurry."

But now Matt was staring off into the distance. "Wathek is returning!" he whispered. "He has to come back!"

Tansy looked at him for a moment. He seemed to have gone into a trance. She shook him violently. "Matt! Matt, don't listen to them! *I* need you!"

Matt shook his head, once lightly and a second time more violently, as if trying to fling something away from him. He rubbed a hand over his eyes, then nodded. Without another word he and Tansy scooped the rest of the bones into the box.

But when they stood to go, they both cried out in horror.

The path back to the door was blocked by a pack of rats. There were nine of them, each as big as a raccoon. Even worse than their size were their eyes—red, beady, and seeming to have enough intelligence to be consciously evil.

Tansy's throat was dry, and she felt a cramp of fear in the pit of her stomach. The rat pack was restless. They were shuffling, and their noses twitched ceaselessly as they evaluated the smell of the two teenagers.

"Tansy . . ." said Matt.

The pack moved forward.

Matt and Tansy stepped back.

"Begging your pardon, miss," said Charity. "Don't you think—"

She was interrupted by a cry from Matt as one of the rats leaped forward and sank its teeth into his thigh.

"Get it off me!" he pleaded, writhing in pain.

The other rats surged forward. Tansy jumped back, stumbled, and fell. For a horrible moment she was lost under a crush of squirming, furry bodies. She began to scream as teeth tore at her arms and legs.

"Your spell, miss!" shrieked Charity. "Use your spell!"

It was instinctive this time. Without thought, without effort, Tansy thrust her hands forward and blasted freezing cold through her fingers.

The first rat she touched froze solid and slammed lifelessly to the floor. Swinging her arms frantically, she dispatched four more rats in a matter of seconds.

Squealing and chittering, the remaining rats withdrew into a half circle, where they stared hungrily at the two teenagers.

With a groan Matt staggered to his feet. He was torn and bleeding in a dozen places. Tansy had fared little better. The whole episode had not taken more than ten seconds, but she, too, had been wounded by the rats' fangs. Blood matted in her hair, and the back of her head ached where it had slammed against the floor.

Charity's bones were scattered in a wide circle.

"Fire should finish them off," said Matt grimly, raising his hands.

"No!" cried Tansy. "Use your flames here, and you're apt to set the whole house on fire. We'll probably get caught and burn to death ourselves. I'll have to use the frost. It's not as bad this time—I didn't get so tired."

Even as she spoke she swayed and almost fell to the floor.

"That's from the bites," she said quickly. "Not from using the spell."

The rats were eyeing them warily. Tansy raised her hands and aimed a blast of frost at the nearest. It squealed and sprang aside. An icy spot formed on the floor, but the rat was safe.

"They've gotten smarter, miss," said Charity.

Tansy tried again, targeting the same rat. But he leaped aside even as she aimed, and once more she missed. Furious now, she blasted out several shots of frost. Squealing with terror, the rats turned and fled into the darkness.

"That's done it, miss!" cheered Charity. "Good for you!"

Tansy staggered and leaned against Matt for support.

"Let's get out of here," he said.

"My bones!" cried Charity. "You can't leave my bones!"

Tansy stopped.

"Tansy!" cried Matt. "For heaven's sake, we can't—"

"We can't leave them, Matt," she replied. Though her voice was weak, it was firm. She knelt and began to gather the scattered skeleton.

"Keep watch, Charity," snapped Matt. "If they start coming back, you tell Tansy. You understand me?"

The ghost nodded meekly.

Glancing about nervously, Matt knelt to help Tansy regather the bones.

"Now my head," said Charity, once they had them all.

"What?" cried Tansy.

"My head. We'll have to bury my head, too. You know where it is."

"What does she want now?" asked Matt anxiously.

"I have to get another box on the way out," said Tansy, deciding to skip the details.

Muttering angrily, Matt hoisted the box of bones, and they started forward again. This time he was the one who stopped. "Did you hear that?" he whispered. "They're coming back."

The rustling died.

Matt and Tansy stood still, waiting for the rats to reappear.

Nothing happened.

They began to walk again.

"Behind you, miss!" cried Charity.

Tansy spun and spotted a rat slinking after them. She raised her hands. The rat dodged, but this time it was too slow. The blast of frost struck it in the hindquarters. It crashed to the floor, its back legs frozen and useless.

Though Tansy had no pity for it, the pained squeals it made as it used its front paws to drag itself across the floor turned her stomach.

"Nice work," said Matt. "Three left."

"If that first pack was all of them," replied Tansy.

They moved forward again. Tansy had a terrible urge to break and run. But she felt certain that if she did, the pack would leap out and catch them before they could use their spells. This slow, careful walking was excruciating, but seemed safer.

They passed the nightstand, and Tansy picked up the box that held Charity's severed head.

They neither saw nor heard the rats again until they had nearly reached the door.

Then the rustling started once more.

"Here they come," said Matt nervously.

Tansy jumped when she saw a dark shape scurry over a pile of boxes. It was followed by another, and then two more.

"Well, there's more than three of them," she said grimly.

Matt nodded, and they continued forward.

The rustling grew louder. Tansy tucked the box under one arm and wiped a hand across her brow to stop the blood from running into her eyes. She saw another shape to her left.

"There's one behind you again, miss," warned Charity.

Tansy swung about. The rat was several paces back.

It was not moving. Another came to crouch beside it. The two creatures glared angrily at her.

Suddenly Tansy realized that they were being herded by the rats, like sheep into a pen.

"Matt, they're all around us."

He nodded. "I know. We'll just have to keep moving."

His face was white, and Tansy suddenly feared that he might not make it to the door. She realized that his shirt was soaked with blood, as was the right leg of his jeans. She had the feeling that the only thing keeping him from falling to the floor in a dead faint was sheer willpower.

"Hold on, pal," she said softly. "We'll get out of this somehow."

"Yeah," he said. "You bet."

They moved forward again, but when they finally spotted the door, Tansy's heart plummeted.

It was blocked by dozens of rats, all of them ready to pounce.

Tansy could see the muscles bunching in the rats' shoulders as they tensed themselves to attack.

"Take the box," whispered Matt.

She turned toward him and placed the wooden box that held Charity's head on top of the box with her bones. Then she took them both back from Matt.

"Hold on," he whispered, raising his hands to shoulder level.

The rats began to stir.

"Okay, watch this!"

Even as he spoke, the rats pounced. But they had waited too long. Fire erupted all around them. A horrible squealing filled the attic as the terrified rodents scrambled to escape the leaping flames. Turning in a rapid circle, Matt continued to gesture, making sure that the circle of flame was complete, that all the rats had fled.

"Come on!" he said, pushing Tansy before him. "We have to get out of here!"

Weak from loss of blood, Tansy staggered as Matt thrust her toward the flames. "Matt!" she cried in horror. "Don't!"

"It's not real! Hurry, before they figure that out!" He continued to push Tansy ahead of him, and new terror filled her as she stumbled into the flames.

Charity was screaming.

The flames roared around Tansy, licking at her face and hands. Yet to her astonishment, she felt nothing.

Reaching past her, Matt opened the door. He thrust Tansy onto the top step, stepped out with her, then slammed the door behind them.

Instantly the air was filled with angry squeals and the sound of heavy bodies slamming against the door. His face grim, Matt braced himself against it. After a moment the pounding stopped, and he relaxed a bit. "I guess they've given up," he said. Putting a hand to his forehead, he swayed just a little.

"What . . . what did you do?" asked Tansy.

He grinned smugly. "I used my *other* power—the spell of illusion. It was enough to convince them—"

Suddenly his eyes rolled back in his head so that only the whites showed. His knees buckled and he began to fall. He grabbed Tansy's arm for support. Weak and off balance herself, she staggered and dropped the boxes. The larger one burst open, and Charity's bones went bouncing down the stairs, flying around Matt as he, too, thumped and bumped his way to the bottom.

Tansy lunged for the box with Charity's head. Grabbing it from where it teetered on the edge of a step, she overbalanced and fell after Matt. She screamed as she rolled down the uncarpeted steps. Battered and jolted, she landed beside Matt at the base of the stairs.

Though she was unconscious, she still clutched Charity's box, which remained securely latched.

It was all too much for Charity, who sat down at the top of the stairs and began to cry.

Matt groaned. He stirred once, lifted his head, then fell back to the floor.

Tansy did not move at all.

So neither of them saw the enormous snake slithering in their direction.

"Oh, miss!" cried Charity. "Wake up, miss. Wake up before it's too late!"

Tansy moaned but didn't stir.

The snake was only a few feet away now. Its head was larger than Charity's, and its eyes glittered with an almost human intelligence.

"Wake up, Miss Tansy!" cried Charity. *"WAKE UP!"*

The snake's body had begun to coil. It raised its massive head from the floor, preparing to strike.

15

COMPULSION

"Gwynhafra!" whispered the Guardian of the Sword. The note of fear in its voice made Denise shudder.

Jenny looked around the room until she spotted Denise. "Niana?" she asked.

"Don't call me that! It scares me."

Jenny looked distressed.

"What happened in there?" cried Derek. "Did you use your spell to open locks? How did you get the rod?"

Jenny turned on him. "There is no time for questions," she said disdainfully. "We must return to the library."

"What do you—"

Her voice was sharp as she cut him short. "To the library!"

She strode forward. As she passed the creature, she shot it an angry glance. It shrank back from her, as if afraid of being struck.

Speechless, the group followed Jenny into the hall.

Suddenly she spun about and lowered the rod.

Derek and Denise turned, too. Denise grabbed Derek's arm and began to scream.

At the end of the hall coiled an enormous snake, forty feet long at least. Its triangular head was raised and ready to strike.

Beyond the snake, at the foot of the stairs, sprawled Matt and Tansy.

The snake hissed and thrashed its tail.

The crystal globe mounted at the end of the rod Jenny was holding made a sizzling sound. Suddenly it erupted with light. A red bolt streaked down the hall. It struck the snake's head, which disappeared in a cloud of vapor. The body writhed violently, smashing against the walls. Green ichor pumped from its neck.

When the thrashing had stopped enough for them to pass, Derek and Denise scrambled down the hall toward Matt and Tansy. Jenny followed at a slower pace, moving as if she were a queen.

Denise dropped to her knees beside Matt, crying out in horror at the ragged rat bites that scored his body. Derek rolled Tansy over and shook her shoulders, trying to wake her.

"Don't waste time with that foolishness," said Jenny in an imperious tone. "Niana, you are a healer. Use your power to help them."

Derek turned to Jenny with bewilderment in his eyes. Denise shot her a venomous glance.

But she began to sing.

Her voice was soft and seemed to come from far away. Though the words were strange to Derek's ears, the tune seemed comforting. As Denise sang, she passed her hands over Tansy's wounds. The flesh closed beneath her fingers, forming angry scars that puckered and then vanished as the song continued.

Tansy moaned and began to stir. Denise turned her attention to Matt.

Fifteen minutes later a strangely assorted group stumbled into the library. Matt and Tansy, their clothes torn but their bodies healed, carried the mortal remains of Charity Jones. Behind them walked Jenny, a strange, serene smile lighting her face. Derek and Denise, who had never been close, now clung to each other like a pair of lost souls. Next in line, invisible to all save Matt, floated a weeping Charity Jones. Lurching along at the end was the creature from the cellar.

"Well, here's your damn ring," said Matt, slapping it onto the table in front of Travis. "And here are Charity Jones's famous bones." He dropped the box onto the table, causing the bones to rattle inside it. "Here's her head, too, if that interests you," he added, taking the box from Tansy. "And there's the rod. If you can get it away from her, whoever she is, you can have it."

Travis looked from face to face. "What's going on?" he asked. His voice sounded so small and helpless that Tansy might have laughed if she hadn't been so scared herself.

"You're not Karno yet," said Jenny in surprise. She looked around at the others. "Where is everyone?"

She stepped away from them and raised the rod above her head. The ball began to glow a smoky red, casting a bloody tinge over everything in the room.

"Karno!" she cried. "Wathek, Niana, Diaz, Theoni. Come to me! Gwynhafra calls!"

The orb at the end of the rod began to pulse, its red light dimming and flaring.

"Stop her!" boomed the creature.

"Karno!" cried Jenny again. "Wathek, Nia—"

Derek lunged against her, knocking the rod from her hands. It clattered to the floor. Its light flickered and died.

"You fool!" hissed Jenny. She raised her hands, but Derek grabbed her wrist, swung her around, then pinned both hands behind her. He looked to the others for help as Jenny struggled against him.

"Your spell, Derek!" shouted Denise. "Use your spell of binding!"

"I don't know how!"

"Travis, help him," said Matt.

Travis stood unmoving, as if too stunned by the chain of events to do anything. Matt shoved him aside and grabbed the game book. He paused. The book seemed somehow larger than it had before. The pages were yellowed, the old-fashioned lettering hard to decipher.

There was no time to worry about that. Jenny was fighting, and Derek was having a hard time holding her. Matt flipped through the pages.

"Here it is!" he yelled. " 'By the power of my staff,

I conjure you to cease all motion.' Those are the words, Derek. Use them!"

Derek repeated the spell. Nothing happened.

"You have to be holding this, you fool," said the creature, snatching the stave from the table with one of its tentacles. "Here, take it!"

Derek had to take one hand off Jenny's wrists to grab the stave. The instant he did, she tried to wrench herself away from him. But as his hand closed over the stave, he repeated the spell.

Instantly Jenny went still, her face stolid and unmoving, her body rigid as death.

Derek stepped away from her, his hand up, ready to reach out if she should move.

She was like a statue.

Travis shook his head as if he were coming out of a trance himself. Looking at Tansy, he said, "You have the power to compel truth. Let's find out what's going on here."

Tansy nodded. The others gathered about her in a tense knot. She stepped forward and stood face to face with Jenny.

"Who are you?" she asked.

"My name is Gwynhafra," answered a voice that was not really Jenny's. It was strange, mournful, distant. Hearing it, the others knew beyond all doubt that Jenny's body was inhabited by someone else.

Tansy hesitated. Fearing the answer, she asked, "Where is Jenny?"

"In here, with me."

"May I talk to her?"

"No! This is my body now, and will be until we make the final crossing. Then she can have it back."

"Is she all right?" asked Tansy.

Gwynhafra didn't answer.

"I said, 'Is she all right?' " repeated Tansy fiercely. Then she added, "I compel you to answer me."

"She is frightened," said Gwynhafra reluctantly.

Uncertain what to ask next, Tansy finally settled on, "Where are you from?"

"Earth."

Acting on an impulse, she asked, "And where else?"

Gwynhafra paused. "Quarmix," she said, after a moment. Her voice was tinged with a note of loathing.

"Ask her where Quarmix is," said Denise.

Tansy repeated the question.

"Far away," said Gwynhafra mournfully. "Very far away, yet very near. It is one of Earth's twins. There are dozens of them, lying side by side, in dimension after dimension. Each is like all the others. Yet each is different, in little ways . . . or big ones. Quarmix is like Earth gone bad. All things there are bitter and twisted—including its people, such as they are."

"How did you get there?" asked Tansy.

Gwynhafra hesitated a third time. Just as Tansy was about to insist on an answer, she began to speak. Eyes glittering feverishly, she poured out the strange story of Erik Karno.

16

COVEN KARNO

"Erik Karno was a scholar," said Jenny/Gwynhafra. "It was his nature, and he never tried to fight it. From as early as he could remember, he had preferred the pursuit of knowledge to all other activities. When he was very young and the other boys played in the street, laughing and yelling, Erik could be found crouched at the feet of the old men, listening to their stories, asking them questions. The elders of the village liked Erik. They were pleased by his intensity. Yet he frightened them with his quickness and his probing questions."

As Gwynhafra spoke, the players felt themselves caught up in the web of her storytelling, her words painting pictures in their minds of a dark time when learning was not easy to come by.

And as they listened, they began to understand Erik Karno's quest for forbidden knowledge.

When he was old enough, Erik entered a monastery—one of the few places in Europe where learning was still given some honor.

He chose this particular monastery for a specific reason. According to rumor, it had once been home to a collection of books that had been outlawed as too dangerous for the world at large. The books had been placed in the care of the monastery, and there were supposed to have been burned. But it had long been whispered that they had actually been preserved by a monk who, like Karno, could not stand to see any book destroyed.

So Karno joined the order, where he spent many years crouched over a tall wooden desk, copying out manuscripts in beautiful flowing script, decorating the pages with his own strange designs and insignia. Often the abbot would reprimand him for his innovations. Yet Erik continued to make them, secure in the knowledge that the reprimands would never amount to more than a scolding, because no other monk worked with such speed and precision, or created such beautiful pages.

The abbey was ancient, dating back to the first thrust of Christianity into Erik's homeland. A place of cold comfort, it was built of stone on a rocky prominence. In winter a demonic wind howled about the walls and towers, and the slate floors were like ice.

Many of the monks died young.

But not Erik Karno. He thrived, because he was

able to do what he loved most: dig into the past and learn things better left forgotten.

His learning took two forms.

The first was a slow learning of special beauty that came from copying manuscripts. Erik would dwell on the texts he copied, savoring every word, examining the connections between them, exalting in the intricacies of sentence and paragraph that unveiled themselves more fully every time he put them onto parchment. Crouched in his lonely cell he brooded over the ideas the manuscripts contained, finding depths of meaning most readers would never have guessed were hidden there.

More secret, and thus even more thrilling, was what he discovered in the catacombs beneath the abbey on the night of his twenty-first birthday.

He had spent the day huddled over his desk, copying an ancient text. When evening came and services were over, he found himself strangely restless. Against the rules, he left his cold stone room and padded down the hallway, past cell after cell, where murmuring monks knelt in self-abasement. He had no destination in mind; he simply knew that he could stay in his own cubicle no longer.

His wandering led him to a stairwell that stretched downward into darkness. Backtracking, he took a torch from one of the pillars in a more traveled area. Then he returned to the stair.

By the flickering light of the torch, he descended into the gloom.

Outside a cold wind howled unmercifully.

Above him a hundred monks settled down to sleep and dream.

Before him a whole new world lay waiting.

At the end of a long stone corridor, he came to another stairway. He followed it down, found another hall, and another stair, and then was enmeshed in the catacombs beneath the abbey. Far older than the abbey itself, the winding passages dated back to a time when pagan tribes had made blood sacrifices in homage to dark powers.

For hours Erik Karno wandered the catacombs. It was well past midnight when he came upon the treasure, a store of wealth that was not beyond his wildest dreams, but was, indeed, an exact match for them. For he had found not gold or silver, but a room filled with books.

His heart leaped at the sight. After finding a rack for his torch, he picked up a dusty, leather-bound volume. Fingers trembling, he turned its pages. His heart leaped with wonder. He snatched up another, and another, and felt himself break into a cold sweat as he knew for certain that he had found the abbey's fabled collection of forbidden lore.

Karno stayed in the chamber until evening of the next day, poring over the banished volumes. Here were answers to questions that had plagued him since the first night he had looked at a dark and starry sky and wondered at the mysteries behind it. Here were the ancients' visions of the world and how it came to be. And here were formulas for power, and methods for calling up dark creatures.

Although he was severely reprimanded for his absence the following day, Karno returned frequently to the secret trove of books until he had learned all he could. Then, carrying several of the most arcane volumes with him, he left the abbey and began to travel darkened Europe.

Though his powers could have made him a wealthy man, he was not interested in money, and used his learning simply to earn a living. In truth, he wanted only two things: to increase his knowledge and to find companionship. So everywhere that Erik Karno went, he looked for others of his kind—others who burned to know the secrets of the universe, no matter how fearsome they might be.

And he found them, in villages and cities, even in the hovels of peasants. It took more than a hundred years, but time had become irrelevant to Erik Karno; death was one of the first barriers his learning had breached. From all across Europe he gathered his disciples. In France he found Niana; in Spain, Diaz. Theoni he took from a Gypsy tribe; she was only three, but a fire in her eyes spoke of what she was, and what she might become.

Extending his search to the borders of Asia, he found Wathek in a mountain village. And last of all, back in his own northern lands, he came upon Gwynhafra.

Gwynhafra was young and beautiful, attributes about which she didn't care, almost didn't notice. Like the others, she was consumed by a passion for learning that had dominated everything else in her life. At least it had until Karno appeared with his band of followers. After that, she had two loves: learning, and Erik Karno.

The band continued to roam Europe. They sought out reputed wise men (who often proved to be frauds) and followed up rumors about other caches of ancient books (which usually proved to be unfounded). They dug through ruins and explored catacombs. They burrowed into the bowels of ancient crumbling castles. And every now and then they found a treasure that made the search worthwhile. This might happen only once in a decade. For Karno and his followers, that was enough.

To pay their way they exorcised ghosts and removed curses.

Yet something strange, something unfortunate, was happening to the group. The more they tampered with power, the more satisfaction they found in using it. What had begun as a quest for knowledge gradually became a quest for strength and mastery, too.

After a time they began to accept money for casting spells. They were amused to find that it paid much better than removing them. No matter where they went, there was someone who wished someone else evil.

Finally Europe began to pale for them. Following the waves of exploration, breaking new paths themselves, they wound their way into the Orient and sought the ancient knowledge of the East. From India to Tibet they wandered, in search of lore and power.

* * *

Gwynhafra paused.

"Oh, no, you don't!" cried Derek. He grabbed her shoulders and furrowed his brow in concentration. For a moment his entire body trembled with the effort he was making.

"There," he said at last. "That will do it for a while. But she's strong—much stronger than I am. I don't know how long I can keep the spell of binding in place."

Tansy nodded. She was aware that the creature seemed to be disturbed. Its tentacles were rippling, its body swelling and contracting. She wondered what was bothering it.

Other than that, all her attention was on Gwynhafra. She didn't see the strange expression on Travis's face.

"What happened next?" she asked.

"It was in the mountains of India that we met our doom," said Gwynhafra, "though we were half a world away before we knew it.

"In the Himalayas there lives a Council of the Wise, chosen to monitor the world and guard it from too much magic. In search of knowledge as always, we visited them, which was *not* wise, for we already had too much magic. The council saw what we had not yet realized ourselves: that while we had barely used that magic in all the centuries we had been gathering it, had scarcely begun to tap the power that was ours, we were growing restless.

"The power, and the knowledge of that power, had begun to gnaw within us. The council knew, even before we did ourselves, that we would soon be making greater and greater magic—not for gain, but simply because we could.

"And when our magic finally threatened to disturb the Great Balance, the Council of the Wise sent Mormekull to stop us. He was our nemesis, and our doom. He tracked us halfway across the world. And with the help of one who should have known better, he brought disaster upon us."

17

ARTHUR GRIMSBY

Gwynhafra's voice was bitter.

"What happened next was not Karno's fault. The rest of us were responsible. We were too anxious to use our power. For Karno himself, the knowing was always enough.

"We heard of the New World and decided to journey here. We did not expect to find great secrets. It was simply someplace new to learn about.

"We left Asia, unaware that Mormekull was on our trail. Our passage was slow because we continued our search for knowledge and power as we traveled westward.

"When we reached England, we stopped for several years to record our journeys. It was there that we first learned of Mormekull and his mission. But our circle was tight, and he could not touch us.

"There, too, we took on a servant.
"His name was Arthur Grimsby."

The creature began thrashing its tentacles, as if greatly agitated. Gwynhafra kept talking.

"That was our greatest mistake, and the source of our downfall. Arthur Grimsby was not one of us. He shared our thirst for knowledge, but not our ability. That made him bitter."

"That's not so!" cried the creature. "You're lying!"

It dropped its voice, and when it spoke again, the tone was indeed bitter. "Or else you never understood."

"Silence!" cried Gwynhafra. "This tale is mine to tell!"

As the gamesters exchanged serious glances, the creature continued to pulsate with agitation. They felt reluctant to look it straight on. Though Gwynhafra was, for the moment, in their power, they sensed she did not want them to look at the creature, and this seemed to restrain their stares—and their questions.

"We had been considering the matter of a servant for some years," she continued. "But we had never found the right person. We needed someone who could stand the traveling, which was often rigorous; someone who could face the mysterious, often terrifying, things that went on around us. We needed someone who could remain silent about what he saw. Most of all, we needed someone we could trust with our very lives.

"Arthur Grimsby *seemed* to be that man.

"I found him in London, running a used-book store. He had a section of volumes on the occult, and though

I did not expect to find anything of interest, I stopped to examine it, as was my habit. Sometimes such places surprise you.

"I knew instantly that Grimsby was different. He had a certain . . . intensity. We talked as he showed me the books and it became clear that he had studied them carefully. He was filled with false knowledge, alas, for the books were mostly nonsense and fakery. But he was intent on learning.

"I spoke to Karno about him, and Karno went to the shop to see for himself what this Arthur Grimsby was like. In time each of us visited him, and examined him in our own way.

"We discussed the matter for months. Finally Karno went back to the shop to make Grimsby an offer.

"The man was thrilled. He joined us immediately.

"For a time all went well. Arthur removed many unnecessary burdens from our shoulders. When it was time to leave for America, he made all the arrangements. His planning was perfect.

"We came to trust him completely. We discussed our secrets in front of him. He had interesting insights, and sometimes his lack of knowledge would help us find a focus for our own questing.

"We were fond of him, so it was terribly painful when he finally betrayed us."

"I did not betray you!" cried the creature. "I was trying to *save* you! I would have given my life for any of you—especially you, Gwynhafra. You know it's true."

Its voice broke, and Tansy was amazed to see tears seeping from the great misshapen eyes.

Gwynhafra turned toward the creature, and her eyes were cold. "You betrayed us, Arthur. You led Mormekull to our home!"

"But tell them why!" the creature shrieked. "Tell them what you were going to do!"

Gwynhafra said nothing.

"What *were* you going to do?" asked Tansy. "I compel you to answer!"

"We had decided to make the New World *our* world; to take it over completely. It would have been easy, for we had the knowledge and the power to do it."

"Yes," cried Arthur, "you did! But it would have cost you your very souls, and you know it. You know it!"

Gwynhafra ignored him and went on.

"When we took ship for America, the idea was just beginning to form in our minds. But when we arrived and saw how crude everything was, how unsettled, we knew we could easily do it."

She sighed.

"It would have been wonderful. We could have made it a place of peace and plenty."

"With everyone else here your slaves!" muttered Arthur. "Don't forget that part."

"A great many of the people here were slaves already," said Gwynhafra sharply. "The country had decided that slavery was an acceptable institution."

She paused, as if gathering her thoughts, then said, "We found a house in New England—a large place, much like this one—where we established ourselves and began to plan." Her voice was sharp now. "But even as we made our plans, we were being betrayed.

"As I said, Mormekull had followed us. But we were well protected by our own spells, and he could not touch us until he found the weak link in our chain—Arthur Grimsby.

"He came to Arthur and slowly poisoned him against us.

"And Arthur let him in."

Now there were tears on Gwynhafra's cheeks as well. For an odd instant Tansy wondered if the tears were for herself—or for Arthur Grimsby.

"Mormekull took us unaware, and he banished us from Earth—from Earth to Quarmix.

"Arthur came to Quarmix with us, though we never knew for certain whether Mormekull had planned it that way all along, or Arthur had simply been caught in his spell."

"And tell them what you did then!" cried Arthur. "Tell them what you did to me!"

Gwynhafra's eyes were blazing now, the cold hate turned to hot rage. "We changed you to what you are now," she hissed. "We gave you a body to match your twisted soul, *betrayer!*"

The creature shook and sobbed. "I loved you! Mormekull told me—showed me!—that you would lose your souls. I couldn't let that happen. I loved you. . . ."

"The fate of our souls was not for you to decide," said Gwynhafra. "You assumed too much, and so you were cast out. Cast into the caves of Quarmix."

"And you would have let me die there!"

"Of course! It was what you deserved. If Mormekull had not come and given you the sword to guard—the sword he stole from us—you would have perished quickly. But betrayal has its rewards, doesn't it, Arthur?"

Arthur Grimsby had closed his eyes. He did not answer Gwynhafra.

"How did you get into Jenny's body?" asked Tansy.

"For nearly two centuries we have monitored Earth, seeking a way back. But the only way to break Mormekull's spell was to re-create the circumstances under which it was cast.

"For a long time it seemed impossible. We tried. We learned to reach past Quarmix and affect the thoughts and actions of people on Earth. But never enough. Never enough.

"Still, we watched carefully, waiting for our chance.

"And finally it came. We saw people begin to play at witches and wizards, pretending to use spells and powers. It struck us that if we could influence someone to create one of these games so that it reflected *our* reality, we could use it as a passage back.

"And that is precisely what we did. Spirits and Spells came to its creator in a series of dreams. These dreams were sent to him from Quarmix, by Coven Karno.

"We have watched, and waited, and tried to put ideas in people's minds—including the thought that it would be fun to play this game in the setting it was designed for.

"And finally we were successful. All the right factors have conjoined. Tonight Earth and Quarmix intersect in this house, in a crossing that grows closer and stronger with every passing hour. Tonight the spell will be re-created."

She paused. When she spoke again, her voice rang with triumph. "And when it is, Coven Karno will return to Earth. Tonight the return. And tomorrow? Ah, tomorrow the planet will be ours!"

18

MASS ATTACK

For a moment no one spoke. Stunned by Gwynhafra's pronouncement, Tansy had no idea what to ask next.

She felt a tap on her shoulder. Turning, she was startled to see one of Arthur's tentacles.

The creature motioned her closer. When she approached, he lifted himself up and whispered in her ear.

Tansy turned to Derek. "Is the binding that holds her still tight?"

He nodded.

Tansy smiled. Then she looked the sorceress in the eyes and said, "I compel from you the truth. Tell me how to free Jenny from your power."

Gwynhafra looked from Tansy to Arthur, her eyes

blazing. She locked her jaw and tipped her head back defiantly.

"I compel you!" said Tansy.

Gwynhafra snarled—there was no other word for the sound that issued from her throat. Her face and neck grew red, and she began to tremble.

"I *compel* you!" cried Tansy.

The snarl turned to a shriek. Jenny's body trembled so violently it was almost as if she were convulsing. Suddenly there was a horrible wrenching sound. The shrieking grew louder, then ceased as Jenny's knees buckled and she collapsed to the floor.

Denise ran forward and knelt at her side.

"Did you know she would do that?" asked Tansy, turning toward the creature. "And is your name really Arthur?"

The creature's face twisted in what Tansy took to be a smile. "Yes, I did, and yes, it is. Arthur Grimsby, at your service. You had Gwynhafra right where you wanted her. She had to answer you. But to do so would reveal her weaknesses. So rather than tell you, she simply fled Jenny's body—giving you what you wanted anyway."

Denise and Derek had helped Jenny to a chair. Denise was singing a healing song to her.

"Are you all right?" called Tansy.

Though obviously shaken, Jenny nodded. "I'm just glad to be back," she said weakly.

"Where were you?" asked Matt. "What was it like?"

"I was right here," said Jenny slowly. "Kind of. I mean, I could see what was going on—hear it all. But it was like I was dreaming. And I had this sense of someplace else behind me." She shivered. "It was bad—a very bad place. And I knew that if something didn't happen, if somehow Gwynhafra didn't get out of my body, I would be stuck in that bad place forever."

She reached out and clutched Derek's hand. "I want to go home," she said urgently.

"We all do," said Derek, his voice uncharacteristically gentle. "We just have to figure out how."

"Well, we have the rod, the ring, the sword, and the stave," said Tansy. "So we can complete the spell. Since everything else from the game has been coming true, I think we can expect that to work, too."

"You're forgetting one thing," said Matt.

"What?"

"The outcome of the game. We've been thinking that we had to win it. But if we win, we free the coven. Remember, we're acting out *their* roles." He shook his head bitterly. "They were playing a game we didn't even know about, and we've fallen right into their hands. We've already done most of what they want. Now if we go ahead and complete that spell, we'll be letting them loose on the world!"

"Yeah, but if we don't, *we* die here at dawn," said Derek.

"Do you think that would really happen?" asked Jenny. Her voice was trembling.

"Yes," said Travis. "I do."

They all looked at him. He was standing behind the library table. Something about the way he had spoken, something strong and powerful, made Tansy uneasy.

"What do you suggest we do?" asked Denise.

"I think we should complete the spell," replied Travis. "The first thing is to get out of here ourselves. And who knows—their powers may not be anything like they claim."

"They sure seem to be so far," said Matt. "What's been going on tonight isn't exactly what you would call normal."

Several of the players began talking at once.

"Be quiet!" yelled Arthur. He was waving his tentacles frantically, and his voice held a note of terror.

The others stopped speaking. "What is it?" asked Denise.

Arthur looked fearfully at the group. "He's here," he said at last, blinking his great drooping eyes. His voice dropped to a whisper. "I can sense him. *Erik Karno is in this room!"*

Tansy felt a chill shiver its way down her spine. Her eyes locked on Arthur, she moved back a few steps and reached for Travis's hand. Slowly the hair on the back of her neck began to rise. She could sense something—*someone*—behind her. "Travis!" she shouted.

He shook his head and blinked. The color drained from his face. "Arthur was right. Karno *is* here." He paused, then whispered, *"He was inside me!"*

The look of terror on his face made Tansy's stomach clench with dread. But before she could think of what to say, what to do, Jenny began screaming.

"No! No, you can't come back. Go away! *Go away!"*

Tansy spun toward Jenny, intending to go help her. But before she could take her first step, it began happening to her, too.

Tansy, crooned a voice in her mind. *Tansy, relax. Let me in. There's so much I can teach you. You've heard our story. You know what this is all about. Let me in, and power beyond your wildest dreams will be yours. Strength will be yours. Knowledge will be yours.*

Tansy clapped her hands over her ears and screamed. It did no good. The voice was coming from inside. She began to beat herself about the head, trying to drive it away.

"Stop!" cried Travis, his voice strong and masterful. He grabbed her wrists.

Tansy looked into his eyes. Travis wasn't there.

"You get out of him, Erik Karno!" she shrieked. "Get out of Travis's body! It doesn't belong to you!"

Again Travis shivered. His eyes rolled back in his head, and his body arched as if an electric current were passing through it. He moaned, and Tansy could tell that Karno was gone.

The room fell silent.

The attack had passed as quickly as it had begun.

But it would come again, and they all knew it. For a moment they simply stood and looked at one another; their eyes haunted, their expressions wary. Each of them was wondering the same thing: Were the others really their old, familiar friends? Or was one—or more—of those faces now merely a mask behind which hid some member of the coven?

Tansy looked at Matt. Was he truly Matt—kindhearted, sharp-tempered Matt, who had been her first boyfriend, way back in seventh grade? Or was he now Wathek, member of Coven Karno? And Denise. Was that really Denise? Or had Niana taken over and simply chosen to remain silent for the moment, letting the others in the coven regroup for their next attack?

She could feel her friends looking at her, and knew they were asking themselves the same questions. She wanted to cry out to them, to say, "I'm Tansy! There's no one else inside me! Theoni has gone!"

But then Theoni was back again, pushing and prodding at Tansy's brain, trying now to accomplish by force what she had failed to achieve with honeyed words. Tansy pulled at her hair, then began pounding her head against the table, hoping the pain would keep her aware, would keep Theoni out. She could hear the others around her, crying out as she was.

The second wave passed as quickly as the first. A moment later the players stood looking at one another even more uncertainly than before.

"Let's do what they want!" cried Jenny. "Let them finish the game and come back. At least we'll get our bodies back when we're done. What difference does it make to us if they escape?"

"You don't understand!" cried Arthur. "You don't know them. Their exile has made them bitter. They are angry now, angry and filled with hate. If you let them into your world, they may well destroy it."

"But we're not strong enough to stop them," said Jenny, pleading, desperate. "Someone else will have to do it. There must be someone who can stop them. We can't do it. We're just kids."

"Maybe someone else can stop them," said Arthur. "But there is no guarantee. You are the first line, and maybe the last. If you don't stop them, it may be too late—for you, and for everyone."

"But how can we resist them?" asked Matt. "I nearly gave in that time, and each attack seems stronger than the one before."

"That's right," said Arthur. "The two worlds are coming together more completely by the moment. The wizards are stronger, wiser than you. But for them to force their way into your minds is unnatural. You have to remember that. They are stronger, but they are going against nature. You do not have their strength, but you have only to keep the balance, not destroy it. So the battle is more equal than you think."

"That's easy for you to say," snapped Jenny. "They're not after you."

Arthur spun about, and two of his tentacles lashed out at her. For a moment Tansy thought he was going to grab Jenny and choke her. "Be quiet!" he hissed. "You don't know what you're talking about. You have no idea—"

"Wait a minute!" yelled Derek. "Where's Travis?"

Tansy spun around. Travis was gone.

And he had taken the objects of power with him.

19

SPIRITS

Travis watched helplessly as his body moved stealthily across the hall. He felt like a marionette, his arms and legs controlled by invisible strings.

That's not a bad simile, said Karno. *In many ways you are my puppet now.*

The words were not spoken aloud; they sounded in Travis's head, coming from the being who had taken over his body.

Travis reacted with a flash of anger. Instantly he was slapped with a burst of psychic pain that would have made him scream in agony, if he had had a mouth to scream with.

Settle down! ordered Karno. *I am in charge for the time being, and you will just have to accept that.*

What are you going to do? asked Travis sullenly.

His words, like those of Karno, were spoken silently in his mind.

I think that should be obvious! We're going to complete the spell.

Karno forced Travis's body to enter a room on the other side of the hall. As they stepped through the door, Travis felt a sudden jolt of memory. He had already been in this room once tonight, while the others were out seeking the objects of power. He had forgotten it until now.

So, you do recall our earlier trip to this room.

I don't understand. You were in control of me then. You must have let go, then taken over again.

Precisely. It's a strain at first, but it becomes easier each time.

The easy contempt in Karno's tone incensed Travis. With a burst of mental energy, he tried to push the wizard out.

Again he felt the slap of psychic pain. *Next time I will not be so gentle,* warned the sorcerer.

Travis forced himself to subside, to wait warily for his chance. He offered no resistance when Karno directed his body to the far side of the room. They stopped beside a tall candelabrum holding seven candles.

Scratched in to the hardwood floor in front of the candleholder was a five-pointed star, inscribed with strange symbols. The star was about eight feet wide.

Looking at it, Travis felt a need to shudder. But his body wouldn't respond, so the shudder stayed trapped inside him, like an itch he could not scratch.

It was about then that he became aware of what

was behind him. Not behind him in the literal sense; it was nothing he could turn around and see. But it was there, waiting for him.

Quarmix.

That's where you'll be going, said Karno pleasantly. *It's a simple one-for-one trade. We remove you to make room for us here—and send you to Quarmix to fill our place there.*

Travis felt a wave of sickness wash over him. This was a kind of fear he had never felt before, a dread that reached to the roots of his soul and made him want to weep.

Because Quarmix was awful.

He was not sure how he knew this. But it was as plain as brown bread, as sure as death. Quarmix was horrible, and horrifying. Now that he was aware of it, it seemed to yawn like an abyss behind him, a great hole toward which he was being forced, inch by slow inch, and into which he must tumble before the night was over, never to return again.

I don't want to go there! he screamed, though not a sound left his lips.

Of course you don't, snapped Karno. *No one* wants *to go to Quarmix. But you'll go when you're sent. You may even survive there. We did. Now be quiet while I make the arrangements.*

He turned toward the door and made a gesture. Though he said nothing, Travis understood that he was sealing the door so no one could enter. He was not exactly reading the magician's mind. It was as though Karno's thoughts *were* his thoughts.

Karno was busy preparing the pentacle for his spell.

He thrust the sword into the floor at the peak of the star. The wood split beneath the blade as easily as a baked potato beneath a table knife. At least two feet of the sword vanished into the floorboards.

The two arms of the pentacle Karno left alone. At its feet he planted the rod and the stave, pressing each about six inches into the solid wooden floor.

Murmuring an incantation, he placed the arm ring in the center of the pentacle.

While Karno worked, Travis tried to regain control of his body. But his arms and legs were no more responsive to his commands than if they had been dead meat.

At the same time he became aware that he had access to Karno's thoughts and memories. He began to sift through them as Karno worked. It was not an easy process—not something he could direct and control. But as scraps of memory floated past, Travis examined them to see what he could learn.

The first thing he found out was that Gwynhafra had spoken the truth. Karno was dedicated to learning.

The second was that he felt an enormous sense of injustice at his banishment to Quarmix.

The third was that he had had experiences more horrifying than anything Travis had ever dreamed of. After briefly tasting a memory of an encounter with angry spirits, and then one with a bloodthirsty vampire in an ancient Albanian cave, Travis decided to leave Karno's memories alone. They were too terrifying to deal with.

Karno was lighting the candles when the shouting began.

"Travis, let us in!" cried Tansy, pounding on the door.

"Unlock that door!" bellowed Matt. "Bring those things back!"

They were joined by the others, an angry chorus demanding to know what he was doing, what he expected to accomplish.

"Who do you think you are, anyway?" cried Denise.

Good question, thought Travis.

Karno smiled serenely at the doorway. *It won't be long now.*

What do you mean?

Wait, said Karno. *Just wait.*

The others were still yelling. "Let us in! Open this door!"

Suddenly their voices began to change.

Travis felt cold fear.

It was no longer his friends calling.

It was Diaz, Niana, Wathek, Gwynhafra, and Theoni.

20

SPELLS

The hallway erupted in chaos as ten spirits fought for control of five bodies, a desperate struggle that was sometimes silent, sometimes grotesquely punctuated by strangled screams and gurgling cries of terror. Charity stood in the doorway of the library, wringing her hands and crying. Arthur was at her side, puffing and swelling as if by anger alone he could turn the course of the battle.

"Erik, let me in!" cried Gwynhafra. "I want to help."

Matt grabbed her shoulder and wrenched her away from the door. "Oh, no, you don't, Gwynhafra!" he roared. "You can't—"

He was unable to finish his sentence. Wathek was making a full-scale attack. His face twisted with effort,

Matt staggered down the hall, trying to drive the intruder from his brain.

Jenny/Gwynhafra grabbed Denise by the arm. "Niana?" she asked hopefully.

"It's Denise!" snarled Denise, slapping her across the face. "Denise!"

For an instant Jenny's expression cleared, as if the blow had expelled Gwynhafra. Then her eyes changed, taking on an expression of rage that could only be Gwynhafra's. But Denise no longer cared. Niana was thrusting at her mind again, tearing the fabric of her sanity with icy fingers.

Tansy watched with horror as Denise began to convulse, and realized that the harder she fought, the worse it was. Soon Denise was rolling on the floor, shrieking and tearing at her hair.

Tansy was trying to wipe away the tears streaming down her own face when Theoni returned. Taking advantage of Tansy's distraction, Theoni took over. Tansy felt as if she had been grabbed by the neck and dragged into a waiting car.

"Let go of me!" she tried to scream. But the scream was silent, because her voice was no longer her own. The lungs and throat that would have produced the sound now belonged to Theoni. Tansy writhed in horror as she raced to the door, felt her fists begin to pound on it, heard her own voice cry, "Erik! Erik, let me in. I'm ready to help!"

She struggled desperately to wrestle control of her body from Theoni. It was like trying to fight with water. She had nowhere to put her efforts. She didn't even know how to *try* to break away.

Though Derek was standing next to her, he was Derek no longer. He was Diaz.

"Stand aside, Theoni," he said gruffly. "I can get in."

Tansy remembered that one of the powers given to Diaz was that of remarkable strength. He drew back a fist, ready to slam it against the door.

"Stop!" bellowed Arthur. He lashed out with a tentacle and wrapped it around Derek's arm. Eyes blazing, Derek turned and grabbed the tentacle with both hands. The muscles in his shoulders bunched as he gave it a ferocious yank.

With a horrible sucking sound the tentacle separated from Arthur's body. His scream was stomach-turning. Derek flung the tentacle away from him. It thrashed around on the floor like an eel out of water, spattering yellowish ooze in all directions. Arthur crouched beside Charity, whimpering and massaging the stump with tips of several other tentacles.

"What did you do that for?" cried Tansy furiously, momentarily wrenching control of her body from Theoni. "He was our friend!" Then her head spun, and she felt as if she had been slapped. Theoni was back in command.

Derek pulled back his fist again. This time he did slam it against the door. The wood shattered, flying in all directions. He stepped through the opening.

"Welcome, Diaz," said Karno. "You have done well."

Inside his body, Travis began to fight again. The words burned on his tongue. He wanted to scream out his anger. But it was trapped inside.

Jenny's body stepped up beside Derek. But it was Gwynhafra who said, "I'm ready, Erik."

Travis/Karno smiled at her.

Derek felt a surge of jealous rage at the deep bond he could sense between Karno and Gwynhafra. Knowing it was not really Jenny who was speaking did nothing to abate his fury. But being under the control of Diaz made it impossible for him to express it.

Matt entered the room. "The boy was strong," he said in a deep voice. "But I have him under control. I'm ready to work, Erik."

"Good," said Karno. "You have done well, Wathek."

Tansy and Denise came in together. "*All* of them were stronger than we expected," said Tansy/Theoni. "They are not as weak-willed as we thought. We will have to work fast."

"Take your places," said Travis/Karno. "It is time to begin."

Moving surely, as if they had practiced this for years, the players took their places around the pentacle. Karno stood at its peak, the candles behind him, the sword between his feet. To his right was Gwynhafra, her blond hair shimmering like hammered gold in the soft light. To Karno's left stood Niana, her dark eyes wide and eager. At the feet of the pentacle, facing their leader, stood Wathek and Diaz, their arms folded over their chests, their faces solemn.

Theoni stood in the center. Karno handed her the golden ring. She slipped it onto her arm, then lifted her hands above her head and cried, "Let the conjuration begin!"

Travis/Karno held a thick book in his hands. It was an old, leather-bound volume, worn from many readings. Tansy understood instinctively that it was, somehow, the same thin game book Travis had read from at the beginning of the evening.

"Let the powers that guard the gates take heed," he intoned. "Coven Karno is here to make the journey between worlds. Let the road from Quarmix be opened."

Lightning flashed above the house, followed almost immediately by an enormous bolt of thunder. The storm raged with new fury. Lightning continued to streak through the sky, one bolt coming almost on top of another, so that the room was lit almost constantly. Eerie shadows flickered over the faces of the six teenagers who had been drawn into a story begun hundreds of years before they were born.

Trapped in her own body, watching through eyes that now belonged to Theoni, Tansy succumbed to pure terror. She had learned two things from the mingling that took place when Theoni was in her body.

The first was how awful Quarmix was.

The second was that when the spell was finished, she and her friends would be trapped in Quarmix forever.

Suddenly she realized that the world was opening beneath her feet. Her cry of horror was heard by no one but Theoni, who did not care at all.

They were standing on the edge of a precipice. Tansy knew that if she fell it would be a fall unlike any other; she would fall clear out of Earth, into the smoking, twisted ruins of Quarmix.

She was silently grateful to Theoni when she stepped back three paces from the edge.

The gratitude quickly turned to renewed terror.

Coven Karno was rising from the center of the pentacle. Their empty bodies stood in a circle, facing outward. Their arms were linked, their eyes cold and dead. And their faces were ravaged by centuries on Quarmix.

Suddenly Tansy understood that when the spell was completed, she and her friends would be free of the spirits. But in that freedom would be their doom. For the coven, once it no longer needed their bodies, intended to compel Tansy and her friends into the center of the pentacle, and from there banish them to Quarmix.

You'd better do something fast, miss!

It was Charity's voice. She was *inside* Tansy's head!

How did you get in here? thought Tansy in astonishment.

I pushed my way in. I had to talk to you, miss. You're in awful trouble!

Tansy could feel Theoni being distracted by the serving girl's presence. It was all she needed—just an instant's break in the witch's concentration. Bursting through, like a swimmer coming to the surface from a deep dive, she took control of her body and screamed, "Travis! Stop them!"

Travis/Karno turned in her direction. The expression of cold fury that twisted his face was more terrifying than anything else that had happened on this insane night. Quickly it gave way to a look of shock. For Travis, deep within, had been touched by Tansy's voice. Taking strength from it, he gained an instant's control over his body and slammed the book shut.

As soon as he did, a tentacle lashed through the air and curled around the book. Wrenching it from Travis's fingers, Arthur held it high in the air.

Travis felt himself submerged again as Karno recovered from his surprise. The wizard's voice was deep and angry. "Arthur Grimsby, if you value what is left of your miserable life, *return that book!*"

The creature laughed. "You've lost, Karno! Admit it!"

"And if I have, where does that leave you?" Karno replied, his voice smooth, caressing. "You betrayed us long ago, Arthur, and you paid a price. But now our exile is over, and yours can be, too. I have it in me to forgive. You cannot know as much as I do, feel as much as I feel, and not have that ability. Give me back the book, Arthur, and all will be forgiven. Give me the book . . . and I will give you back your shape."

The creature quivered, and Tansy could see the indecision in his eyes. She wanted to cry out to him, to urge him to ignore the wizard's honeyed pleading. But her mouth was not her own, and her lips would not form the words.

Karno reached out with Travis's hand. "The book, Arthur," he said, his voice soft, sweet. "Give me the book."

Arthur Grimsby turned to look at Jenny/Gwynhafra. Longing filled his eyes.

She spoke to him, and to everyone's astonishment, it was with Jenny's voice. With clear strength she whispered, "Do the right thing, Arthur."

Then her body spasmed as Gwynhafra seized control once more.

But Arthur Grimsby had made up his mind. Cracking his tentacle like a whip, he thrust the book into the candle's flames, crying, "You've lost, Karno. Now go back to Quarmix!"

An explosion rocked the room as magic clashed with magic and the book erupted in a supernatural blaze. Arthur screamed in agony. Dropping the book, he curled his tentacle back to his mouth.

When the book struck the floor it burst into pieces, spewing flames in all directions. The drapes caught fire. Almost instantly they became two columns of flame blazing behind Travis's head.

The six members of the coven cried out in rage and sorrow as their plans, their centuries of waiting and plotting, vanished into smoke.

Tansy felt a sudden wrenching inside. For an instant, she thought she had been kicked in the stomach. Then she realized that Theoni was gone!

She looked at the others. Their faces were clearing. They were dazed, but free.

They heard a last angry scream, echoing above them, below them, from all sides—an emanation of hate and fury that would haunt their dreams for years to come. Then, with a roar like a collapsing dam, the coven was gone, and the road to Quarmix was sealed.

Tansy turned toward the door to flee.

It was blocked by leaping flames.

21

INFERNO

The flames spread with supernatural speed, the room quickly becoming an inferno.

Thick smoke curled from the center of the pentacle. After a moment it formed into a column.

In the column loomed a black-robed figure.

"Wathek!" cried Matt.

The figure glanced about the room, briefly locking eyes with each player, then moving on. His voice whispered in their minds: *You must pay for defying the coven. So stay. Stay and burn!*

They felt their bodies grow stiff as their arms and legs fell useless under Wathek's spell.

Suddenly Travis's voice rang out. "Karno, I know you! I've seen inside you. This isn't you. *This isn't your way! Do something. DO SOMETHING!*"

For a moment time seemed to stop, the tongues of flame freezing in place. Then a second form appeared in the center of the pentacle. Like Wathek, he wore a black robe. Reaching up, Erik Karno pulled back his hood. His face was at once ancient and young. His dark eyes were pools of bitterness—until he smiled, when they suddenly seemed to hold a secret older than time, deeper than thought, stranger than life itself.

"I release you," he said.

Then, wrapping an arm around Wathek, he disappeared.

Karno had released them from Wathek's spell but not from the chamber of fire.

With a roar the flames came back to life, licking at the walls. Fumes filled the room, making everyone cough and gag.

Tansy felt herself choking on poisonous gases. Sweat poured down her face and arms. The floor beneath her became unbearably hot as tongues of flame leaped between the boards.

Certain that death was near, she began to weep. "Travis!" she cried, "Travis, I—"

Her words were cut off as a tentacle grasped her about the waist, squeezing out her breath. She felt herself lifted from the floor. For a horrible moment she dangled above the flames, felt them licking at her arms, her legs, her face. Then she was sailing through the air.

She struck the wall on the far side of the hallway and slid to the floor, choking and sobbing, gasping for air. Denise was beside her. An instant later Jenny hurtled from the room, followed shortly by Derek, and then Matt.

Tansy waited for Arthur to throw Travis clear of the flames.

Nothing happened.

"Arthur!" cried Tansy, struggling to her feet. "Arthur, where's Travis?"

"I can't find him!" yelled the monster. His voice was desperate—and weak. "The smoke is too thick. I can't see anything!"

"Get out!" cried Jenny. "You have to get out of there now!"

"No!" screamed Tansy.

Denise grabbed her arm. "He has to," she whispered fiercely. "If he doesn't, he'll die, too!"

Tansy began to sob. Denise put her arms around her and held her close.

"Arthur!" cried Derek. "Get out!"

"I can't! I can't get past the flames."

"Reach out to us!" yelled Matt. "We'll pull you!"

Side by side, Matt and Derek stood in front of the door, coughing and gagging as the smoke filled their lungs. A moment later two tentacles came thrusting through the flames. Each of the boys grabbed one.

"We've got trouble," said Matt. Though Arthur's tentacle was wrapped around his forearm, the monster's grip was dangerously weak.

"Just pull!" yelled Derek.

They braced their legs and began to tug. It felt as if they were dragging a dead weight. Matt glanced at Derek. "Do you think we've lost him?"

"Just pull!" repeated Derek fiercely.

They braced their feet and drew even harder. Suddenly Derek fell backward. The tentacle he had been holding came flying through the doorway like a rubber band that has snapped after being stretched too far. Yellow ooze dripped from the severed end.

"Arthur!" cried Derek. He leaped to his feet and rushed into the flaming room.

"Matt, keep pulling!" screamed Denise. She stepped in beside him and hauled on the tightly stretched tentacle. Suddenly a large, lumpish form appeared in the doorway.

"Pull!" cried Denise again.

Arthur was halfway through the door now. Derek stood behind him, desperately trying to push him the rest of the way. Arthur's body was holding down the flames. It made a horrible hissing sound.

"Pull!" cried Denise a third time, and then Arthur was through the door. Derek, soot-smeared and blistered, came scrambling after him.

"His tentacles!" yelled Tansy. "We've got to get his tentacles out!"

All five players began hauling at Arthur's outstretched tentacles. Tansy felt sick. The usually slimy skin was dry and blistered; in places it was cracking, showing the muscle underneath. She hauled out one tentacle and then another. When the third came through the door, she saw that it was clutching the golden sword.

The hallway was starting to fill with flames.

Tansy reached for another tentacle and found they were all free.

She looked at Arthur. The creature's eyes were closed, and he was gasping for breath. His whole body was charred and blistered. The stumps where he had lost tentacles were still oozing. Jenny knelt on the floor beside him, cradling the top of his head in her lap.

"You saved us," she said softly. "We owe you our lives."

"I failed," gasped the creature. "I couldn't save Travis."

"Shhh," whispered Jenny. "You did the best you could. The rest of us would all be dead if it weren't for you."

Tears seeped from beneath the creature's eyelids.

Tansy knelt beside him. Inside she was screaming, aching over Travis. But she knew Arthur had done more than anyone could ask. Touching him gently, fighting to get the words past the lump in her throat, she said, "It's all right. I understand."

"We've got to do something for *him* now," said Denise. "He needs help."

"Quarmix," said the creature softly. "Get me back to Quarmix. In my cave I'll be safe. In my cave I have things that can heal me."

"How?" cried Tansy. "How can we get you back?"

His eyes flickered open. "The armband," he gasped. "Give me the armband."

Startled, Tansy realized she was still wearing the golden armband Theoni had put on while they stood in the center of the pentacle. She slipped it off her arm and extended it to Arthur. Feebly he wrapped the tip of a tentacle around it, then placed it on the floor in front of him.

"This wasn't enough for all of them," he said. "But it will get me home." Painfully he dragged the sword along the floor until it lay across the armband.

Tansy watched him nervously. The flames were getting worse. They didn't have much time.

"Quarmix," gasped Arthur. "Let me return to my home in Quarmix!"

The sword began to glow with an eerie golden light. A ringing sound filled the air around them, louder even than the roar of the flames.

The armband began to grow.

Tansy jumped back. An opening had appeared beneath the expanding armband. Arthur's tentacles dangled over the edge of it.

"Quarmix!" gasped Tansy, looking into the hole.

The five of them stood and watched the ring expand.

"It's the cave," said Derek suddenly. "The cave we saw in the cellar."

"It's home," said Arthur, dragging his body toward the opening. "Help me," he gasped.

The teens gathered around him, pushing and pulling the burned, bulging body toward the gateway to Quarmix. Arthur shuddered with pain, but said nothing until he was nearly over the edge, when he whispered, "Thank you. I will never forget you. I will—"

The hole closed over him with a snap.

He had taken the sword with him. The rod and the stave had been burned. Only the armband, which had shrunk back to its original size, was left.

Tansy reached down and picked it up.

"Come on," cried Derek. "We've got to get out of here!"

He headed for the stairwell. The others followed close behind.

The top steps were bathed in flame.

"No choice!" Derek yelled. "Follow me!"

He plunged into the flames and was lost from sight.

Jenny hesitated and Tansy could see she was not going to make it on her own. "Come on!" she said. Grabbing Jenny around the waist, she rushed through and began to run down the steps.

It wasn't as bad as she had feared. The top of the stairway was the worst part. Flames were leaping out all around them. But below it was a clear path. She could hear Matt and Denise coming down behind her.

It took only seconds to reach the bottom of the steps.

The foyer was filled with flames.

Denise arrived beside Tansy almost instantly. Looking back, she caught her breath. "Matt!" she cried. "Jump!"

Matt threw himself into the air. Even as he did, the stairwell collapsed beneath him. Flames rushed up. A cloud of sparks scattered outward.

Matt hit the floor beside Denise and collapsed in a heap.

Tansy and Denise reached down to help him up.

"No, get down here," gasped Matt. "The air is better by the floor."

Tansy dropped to her knees and crawled along the

floor behind Matt, wincing as the floorboards seared her hands and knees. A beam fell from the archway that led to the dining room. Hot air rushed past her. She felt as if her lungs would catch fire next.

Derek crouched by the front door, waiting.

"Hurry!" he rasped. "Hurry!"

As he saw Tansy emerge from the smoke and flames, he stood and grabbed the doorknob. For a terrible instant Tansy wondered if the door would open, or if it was still sealed.

It opened.

Cool air rushed in.

Morning had never looked so good.

It was still raining, but the thunder and lightning had stopped. Tansy put her hands on her cheeks. The cool water felt more delicious than anything she could remember.

She stood with the others, about fifty feet from the house. She could hear a siren wailing in the town below. The firefighters would be here soon, but they would be too late. The place was like a gigantic bonfire, flames stretching up from all the windows, bursting from the turrets.

Tansy felt tears begin to stream down her cheeks, mingling with the raindrops. "Travis," she whispered. "Oh, Travis—"

Denise put an arm around her. Tansy buried her face in her friend's shoulder, sobbing hopelessly.

"There it goes," said Derek softly.

Tansy looked up.

Slowly, almost delicately, like a house of cards falling in slow motion, the Gulbrandsen place began to crumble. Then the roof caved in, and flames rolled up against the sky.

After that everything moved faster. It was only a matter of seconds before the five watchers recoiled as the house plunged in on itself, and waves of heat rolled out around them.

To their right the sun was just peeking over the horizon.

" 'This house dies at dawn,' " whispered Jenny. She stopped herself, leaving the rest of the curse unspoken. But Tansy's mind, treacherous and willful, filled in the missing words: " 'Along with everyone still in it.' "

The bushes at their right began to rustle. "There you are!" shouted a familiar voice. "I've been looking all over for you!"

"Travis?" cried Tansy, spinning around. *"Travis?"*

He came pushing through the bushes, bruised and smeared with soot, but very much alive. With a little cry she ran to him, threw her arms around him. He held her tight.

Standing behind him was another figure.

"Charity!"

The serving girl smiled. "Yes, miss."

"But I can see you!"

"So that's what she looks like," said Derek appreciatively. "Not bad!"

Jenny elbowed his ribs.

"She saved me," said Travis. "When the fire got out of control, the flames made a kind of wall and I was cut off from the rest of you. Suddenly Charity was standing there, motioning to me to come with her." He paused. "I was a little spooked when I saw her. But I figured anything was better than burning to death."

"I knew another way out of the room!" explained Charity. "There are—were—a lot of old passages and secret doors in the house. Mr. Gulbrandsen liked things like that. We couldn't get back to you, because of the fire. So we had to go out another way. Did I do all right, miss?"

"Charity, you did great!" said Tansy, so weak with relief she could hardly stand.

The ghost smiled, her face radiant. "I knew I had to let Travis see me in order to save him. So I just concentrated as hard as I could. All of a sudden I heard a little pop, and there I was!" Her face grew very serious. "But I have to go now."

Tansy wiped rain and tears from her eyes. "What do you mean?"

Charity smiled again, a softer smile, sweet and gentle. "I'm fixed, miss."

Tansy could hear deep joy in her voice, a note of satisfaction and success. "It wasn't my missing bones that kept me here after all. It was the wicked things I did. But now I've done good. I've helped you folks out and I feel better. So I can go."

"Oh, Charity!" cried Tansy. "I'm so glad for you!" She paused, then said, "But I'll miss you."

"I'll think of you often, miss," said Charity softly.

She began to fade. They could see the world shining through her.

"Good-bye," said Matt, his voice husky. "Good

luck." He blushed. It seemed like a foolish thing to say. But what else could you say to a ghost that was leaving?

"Good-bye!" called Charity. "Good-bye!"

And then she was gone.

Travis turned to Tansy. He took her hand.

In the distance sirens were screaming, drawing closer.

"Let's go," he said. "We'll deal with all that later."

Two by two, they headed east, into the sunrise.

Another Hodder Children's book

SPIRIT WORLD
RESTLESS SPIRITS

Bruce Coville

Lisa Burton and her little sister Carrie can't wait to leave Sayers Island. The weather is terrible and they're bored stiff. But one rainy afternoon their grandmother teaches them 'automatic writing' to pass the time – and now the girls can't stop . . .

But the fun soon turns to terror as angry ghosts confuse the living with the dead and, unless Lisa can find a way to bring peace to the restless spirits, the ghosts will claim the ultimate price for tampering with the unknown – her sister . . .

Another Hodder Children's book

SPIRIT WORLD
EYES OF THE TAROT

Bruce Coville

When Bonnie McBurnie begins to use the ancient deck of tarot cards she found in her grandmother's attic, she taps into a power unlike anything she's ever imagined.

Soon the ancient forces of the tarot begin to haunt Bonnie's life, forcing her to face a fearful secret buried in her own past – and the terrifying wrath of a powerful sorceror who has been waiting centuries for his chance to return.

Can Bonnie master the cards – or will their strange power destroy not only her, but everyone she loves?

Another Hodder Children's book

SPIRIT WORLD
CREATURE OF FIRE

Bruce Coville

The night before her death, Marilyn's eccentric Aunt Zenobia asks her to care for an ancient amulet. But her aunt is handing her more than just a strange piece of jewellery – she's handing her a passport to a terrifying new world. And it may be a one way trip. Faced with an ancient curse, a tragic demon and a blood feud thousands of years old, Marilyn must make the right decision – or die . . .

Another Hodder Children's book

ALIENS ATE MY HOMEWORK

Bruce Coville

Do you have problems telling lies?
Can you only speak the truth – no matter how silly?
Then you'll know how Rod felt when his teacher asked about his science project – because he could only tell her the truth: 'Aliens ate my homework, Miss Maloney!'

Of course, nobody believes Rod, so nobody bothers to ask where the aliens come from. Just as well – because Rod is helping Madame Pong and the crazy crew of the Ferkel on a very secret mission . . .

ORDER FORM

Bruce Coville

0 340 71458 1	Spirit World 1: Restless Spirits	£3.99	❑
0 340 71459 X	Spirit World 2: Spirits and Spells	£3.99	❑
0 340 71460 3	Spirit World 3: Eyes of the Tarot	£3.99	❑
0 340 71461 1	Spirit World 4: Creature of Fire	£3.99	❑
0 340 65115 6	Aliens Ate my Homework	£3.99	❑
0 340 65116 4	I Left my Sneakers in Dimension X	£3.99	❑
0 340 65355 8	Aliens Stole my Dad	£3.99	❑
0 340 63593 2	Goblins in the Castle	£3.99	❑

All Hodder Children's books are available at your local bookshop or newsagent, or can be ordered direct from the publisher. Just tick the titles you want and fill in the form below. Prices and availability subject to change without notice.

Hodder Children's Books, Cash Sales Department, Bookpoint, 39 Milton Park, Abingdon, OXON, OX14 4TD, UK. If you have a credit card, our call centre team would be delighted to take your order by telephone. Our direct line is 01235 400414 (lines open 9.00 am–6.00 pm Monday to Saturday, 24 hour message answering service). Alternatively you can send a fax on 01235 400454.

Or enclose a cheque or postal order made payable to Bookpoint Ltd to the value of the cover price and allow the following for postage and packing:
UK & BFPO – £1.00 for the first book, 50p for the second book, and 30p for each additional book ordered up to a maximum charge of £3.00.
OVERSEAS & EIRE – £2.00 for the first book, £1.00 for the second book, and 50p for each additional book.

Name..

Address..

....

....

If you would prefer to pay by credit card, please complete:
Please debit my Visa/Access/Diner's Card/American Express (delete as applicable) card no:

Signature..

ExpiryDate...

ORDER FORM

More H Supernatural title to look out for from Hodder Children's Books

0 340 68076 8	NIGHT PEOPLE *Maggie Pearson*	£3.99 ❑
0 340 69371 1	THE BLOODING *Patricia Windsor*	£3.99 ❑
0 340 68300 7	COMPANIONS OF THE NIGHT *Vivian Vande Velde*	£3.99 ❑
0 340 68656 1	LOOK FOR ME BY MOONLIGHT *Mary Downing Hahn*	£3.99 ❑
0 340 68331 7	THE GRAVE-DIGGER *Hugh Scott*	£3.99 ❑
0 340 68751 7	NIGHT WORLD 1: SECRET VAMPIRE *Lisa J Smith*	£3.99 ❑

All Hodder Children's books are available at your local bookshop or newsagent, or can be ordered direct from the publisher. Just tick the titles you want and fill in the form below. Prices and availability subject to change without notice.

Hodder Children's Books, Cash Sales Department, Bookpoint, 39 Milton Park, Abingdon, OXON, OX14 4TD, UK. If you have a credit card, our call centre team would be delighted to take your order by telephone. Our direct line is 01235 400414 (lines open 9.00 am–6.00 pm Monday to Saturday, 24 hour message answering service). Alternatively you can send a fax on 01235 400454.

Or enclose a cheque or postal order made payable to Bookpoint Ltd to the value of the cover price and allow the following for postage and packing:
UK & BFPO – £1.00 for the first book, 50p for the second book, and 30p for each additional book ordered up to a maximum charge of £3.00.
OVERSEAS & EIRE – £2.00 for the first book, £1.00 for the second book, and 50p for each additional book.

Name...

Address...

....

....

If you would prefer to pay by credit card, please complete:
Please debit my Visa/Access/Diner's Card/American Express (delete as applicable) card no:

Signature...

ExpiryDate...